This is a work of fiction. Nar
incidents are either the product o
are used fictitiously, and any res‹
living or dead, business establish
entirely coincidental.

Published by Stuart Kenyon 2019

Copyright© Stuart Kenyon 2019

Stuart Kenyon asserts the moral right to be identified as the author of this work.

Cover design by The Book Khaleesi
www.thebookkhaleesi.com

For Vicky, Max and Poppy

With thanks to Mistral Dawn

Chapter 1

'Guess it was inevitable,' John said. Scanning the south wall through his binoculars, he saw the fingers of a single hand. Its knuckles were cracked, the fingernails chipped.

'Your views are noted, sir.' Winston's voice was monotonous.

'I'm sure they are. As always.'

A second hand appeared, scrabbling for purchase. The razor-wire proved no deterrent. Soon a head emerged above the parapet. Briefly John looked into the dead eyes, adjusting the binoculars. Scarred cheeks, fish-like lips, slack jaw, chipped teeth. A year ago, the sight would've terrified John, especially if it arrived at twilight. But by now the zomb-aug's arrival was no more than an irritation, the gloom merely an impediment to timely extermination. Of course, he wouldn't be as cool if it got too close.

Something about the being's appearance disturbed him, though. Illuminated by the twenty metre high floodlights, its flesh and clothes had a silver finish. 'An EMP should do it,' John said, trying to convince himself. He didn't like the metallic sheen; it disturbed and confused him in equal measure.

'Yes, sir.' Winston trundled away. A moment later he returned with a box of grenades, which he gave to his master.

'The launcher?' John sighed and shook his head.

'Yes, sir.' The robot repeated his journey, then loaded the gun with ammunition, his movements mechanical but swift.

Taking the weapon with one hand, John frowned. 'There may be more of them. They don't usually come alone.' He opened the hatch wider and pointed the grenade launcher at the zomb-aug, which had untangled itself from the wire and was about to climb to the courtyard below. It was thirty metres from the south tower to its closest perimeter wall. An easy shot for a man of John's experience. A direct hit was not necessary, either. As long as the EMP detonated within five metres of its target, the shambling figure would stop moving, permanently. Holding his breath, John pulled the trigger.

The dull *whoomp* of the launcher was followed almost instantaneously by the crackle of the grenade exploding as it hit the lip of the wall. But not, as expected, by the sound of a body landing on the floor ten metres below. Unaffected by the electromagnetic pulse which should have fried the circuits powering its undead limbs, the zomb-aug began its descent.

'Shit.' John shook his head and clicked his tongue as he watched the humanoid reach the ground. Sweat needled his brow and the small of his back. His stomach flipped. 'We need a drone.'

The robot scooted away. A moment later he reappeared, a remote control with visual display in hand.

Muttering an unnecessary 'thank you,' John turned away from the viewing hatch to focus on the device Winston had retrieved. Its screen came to life. A couple of swipes and thirty seconds later, the south courtyard was visible on the display. The image vibrated a little; perhaps the robot's camera had come loose. A whirring noise, audible via the open window, grew in intensity as the unmanned aerial vehicle answered its summons.

John wiped perspiration from his upper lip. Using the UAV's video feed, he studied the zomb-aug. When it reached the tarmac, an alarm sounded, and an accompanying light flashed on John's wrist-com. He dismissed the alert and piloted the drone to within ten metres of the zomb.

Resembling a meerkat from a nature hologram, the invader stood straight, seemingly aware of a threat. It swayed for a moment as if undecided. Then it lurched towards the south tower.

Before the zomb-aug could take more than a half-dozen steps, John highlighted its form on the control pad's screen and hit a red button.

Nothing happened. Other than a rapid clicking sound, there was no evidence that John had pressed "fire."

The zomb cocked its head, then started towards its would-be killer's position. Its gait was ungainly, its arms like a puppet's. But it moved with purpose and speed.

'Fuck.' John jabbed the trigger button harder. As if doing so would make any difference. Lips quivering, he watched the UAV's footage.

Its targeting system was still functional. It followed the zomb-aug, who soon reached the south entrance and began to pound on the steel door.

John winced and looked to Winston for inspiration.

The machine provided none.

Suddenly, without warning, gunfire rattled. The monster twitched for a few seconds before collapsing.

Startled, John blinked, still staring at the camera feed. After a moment he recalled his hunter-drone and opened the view hatch to look at his fallen foe. Only then did he exhale in relief. 'Fuck me, that was intense.'

'The drone's guns jammed again,' Winston said.

'No shit.' Affecting insouciance, John continued, 'Like I was saying, I guess it was inevitable.'

'That is a duplicate statement, sir,' the droid observed, unmoved by the drama.

'I know, Winston. That's why I said "like I was saying."'

'Yes, sir.'

'And why do you still call me "sir," Winston?' John closed the window and opened the trapdoor. Down the stairs he went, his electric-powered companion in pursuit. 'I programmed that out, I'm sure I did.'

Winston moved ahead of his creator, as programmed, when they reached the ground floor. 'Should I answer your "guess it was inevitable" observation, or your question about my calling you "sir," sir?'

'Fuck it, Winston, just open the door and let's get that corpse inside and off the grid. Before we have a dozen of the bastards climbing the walls.'

As a pair they dragged the zomb-aug across the yard, the task as distasteful as ever. When they reached the south door, John breathed on the DNA scanner and tapped his foot as the portal opened. A light drizzle had begun to fall; it was cold. He needed to begin his work on the cyborg.

First things first, however. Why was the zomb-aug immune to the EMP?

'We'll take it to the lab, Winston,'

They loaded the body onto a trolley. John led the way, while Winston pushed the gurney.

The laboratory needed a thorough spring clean. Oh well, he wasn't expecting visitors, John thought, smiling wryly. He conducted an examination of the cadaver, wincing when he got blood from the gaping head wound on his polyurethane gloves. The internal electrics, which were originally installed to lend superior strength, speed and stamina to normal human limbs – but now reanimated dead ones – were undamaged. As was the CPU chip located at the base of the skull.

As John worked, he noticed that his hands were becoming coated with a shiny, viscous substance. It mixed with the blood to create a grainy paste. The skin and three-piece suit had been sprayed with an adhesive metallic paint of some sort. By covering the creature's surface area with a conducting material, a Faraday cage had been created, rendering the zomb-aug invulnerable to EMP attack.

Said conclusion posed two worrying questions:

How many of the zombs were similarly protected?

Who'd applied the paint?

'I think we might be in trouble.' John removed his gloves and sat on a chair next to the examining table. He ran his hands through his greasy hair, wondering when he'd last used the hygienosphere.

Winston, who'd switched to "sleep" mode, blinked into life. 'Immediate trouble, or potential trouble, sir?'

'Potential. We'll run out of ammo for the drones, and as we've just seen today, some of them are unreliable. But I reckon we can find a work-around for the EMPs.'

Winston waited.

'But who the fuck is making these things harder to kill? And why?'

'I do not know, sir.'

'I know you don't, I'm just theorising. I'd always just thought the zomb-augs were mindless, wandering around, looking for survivors. But this paint business suggests that someone's in control. Someone's using these bastards for something.' John sighed. 'Fuck knows what.'

'Who is "fuck," sir?'

John laughed. 'You know what, Winston, sometimes I think you're taking the piss. And you're smarter than you let on.'

The robot's face, a poor imitation of a man's if truth be told, was as expressionless as ever. For a moment his eyes remained focussed on John. And then, presumably, his operating system judged the conversation to be over, because he returned to his resting stance. 'Is there anything else you would like to discuss?'

'Plenty, but I don't think I'll get much "discussion" from you, Winston. Anyway, I'd like you to record some thoughts.'

'Certainly, sir.'

'I was saying before that it was inevitable.' John stood and fiddled with a control terminal on one wall, adjusting the air composition by increasing the chlorine inlet, in order to disinfect the chamber. 'I meant the augmentation programme was doomed to failure. Whether it was anarchists who spread the virus, or the AI Council, or whoever, doesn't really matter. It was bound to fuck up at some point.'

'Your views are noted and recorded, sir.'

'I'd like to say I'm glad I opted out of augs, but is this existence,' he signalled his general environs, 'any better than being one of these things?'

'You have asked this question already, sir. May 25 2066 at 1400 hours approximately. My response at the time was —'

'Forget it, Winston. Please dispose of the body and then power down.'

***

Later, John lay in his bunk, unable to sleep. Of course, he could've injected opiates into the air supply and drifted into blissful ignorance, but he was becoming too dependent on narcotics.

His earlier train of thought – that survival was perhaps no less an evil than zombification – was idling noisily in the station of his mind. Life nowadays was more pointless than he'd ever known. Every day he rose. Every day he went to bed. Most days he repelled zomb-augs. Most days he considered permitting them entry to the installation. What would the beasts do to him? What was the worst case scenario?

Not death. John's life was of consequence to no one but himself, after all. They might maim him, leave him to die a slow, agonising death, unable to reach an air-conditioning panel and fill the room with merciful toxins. Unlikely but terrifying nonetheless. Hopefully, one day, when his EMPs were spent and his UAVs disabled, the zombs would kill him quickly. Evidence he'd collected from CCTV cameras elsewhere in the city, and the fates of the few survivors he'd known over the last couple of years, suggested that his eventual demise would be gory but rapid.

Don't go there, he told himself. Don't think of the carnage. The dismemberment —

Don't. Go. There.

Leave that section of your brain shuttered, quarantined, starved of light. At some point, he would finish building Winston's replacement. The new android was to be capable of brain surgery, including the ability to transact memory adjustments. The dark recesses of John's mind would be flushed and cleansed, scoured and scourged. An enema for the soul, it would be.

'Fucking idiot,' John said with passion. Had he learnt nothing? As soon as humans allowed machines to infiltrate their governments, their communities, even their bodies, the consequences were inevitable. A few, John included, had showed foresight by declining augmentation.

Certainly, it hadn't felt like wisdom at the time, as abstention meant marginalisation, loss of employment, separation from family; he was suddenly inferior to his augmented peers. They boasted constant cellular connection to their fellow augmentees. They communicated in an instant, able to read each other's minds, almost. They were walking encyclopaedias, constantly linked to the Internet. They could even manipulate their own body chemistry by using adrenaline or endorphins, testosterone or oestrogen at will. Aug-frees remained human. Weaker mentally and physically, less in control over their own faculties.

But John had made the right decision, ultimately. He wasn't about to surrender to digitalisation now just to spare himself a few bad dreams.

He climbed out of bed and stared out of the window. The skyscrapers, monuments to man's ambition, were still there on the horizon, visible by moonlight. The thousands of windows therein and the streets below were dark, though. Homo sapiens was born of fire, the ability to create light and warmth differentiating humans from beasts. That fire had been all but extinguished. People had become too clever for their own good, and they'd birthed a monster. Like Prometheus, the great minds of the 21st Century had offended the gods. They were being punished accordingly.

John turned away from the empty skyscape and contemplated his gloomy, meagre quarters. His holo-jector, hygienosphere, control terminal. He looked at the 3D live

CCTV feed, at the network of corridors, laboratories, offices, plant rooms, shop floors. Most were disused, but all were under his command. The security, air composition, ambient temperature, lighting, all his to direct as he saw fit. This was his domain. And although the former headquarters of Asquith Robotics was not a grand fortress, it was safe, well-stocked with weaponisable hardware and victuals, and it was manageable.

John controlled technology. It didn't control him. When the malware was distributed, a little under two years ago, there had been no parasitic operating system in his head. The virus had passed him by. He'd survived while others expired and were resuscitated, their new identities a mockery of humanity.

For a few minutes, John watched the 3D camera feed, as was his habit before retiring. A last glance at his wrist-com confirmed that the device was functional and ready to alert when necessary. Whilst closing his window blinds, a flicker of movement in the distance arrested his attention. 'What the fuck….' he breathed. Amidst the high-rises was a plume of smoke, which rose and drifted eastwards. Impromptu explosions were not uncommon; fuel cells expired, and unmaintained chemical storage sites surrendered to time. However, the resulting conflagrations were typically more spectacular. This appeared man-made, the starved optimist in John asserted.

Perhaps he was not as alone as he'd presumed.

Chapter 2

Not for the first time, John had misjudged the proportion of tranquillisers in his nocturnal respiratory prescription. He woke groggy, but at least he'd had no nightmares. Naturally, it was a mistake he tried to avoid, because had he received visitors during the night, he would've been ill-equipped to dispose of them. Yet his wrist-com was dormant; the klaxons were silent. John's fiefdom remained unbreached.

He took deep breaths of the caffeinated air for a few minutes, savouring the buzz. And then he remembered the smoke. His first thoughts, giddied by the stimulants in his blood, were of expedition, of going forth and multiplying. There might be women out there. It'd been so long since he'd touched a woman, caressed warm, supple skin, sampled the nectar of —

'Shit, John,' he admonished. 'Too much caffeine always does this.'

First things first. When living in a world largely populated by fearsome zombies intent on one's death, there were five priorities: security, security, security, security, everything else. John spoke into his wrist-com, 'Awake, Winston.'

Moments later, the robot arrived. 'Good day to you, sir.'

'Hello, Winston. And how are you on this fine morning?'

'All my systems are fully operational, sir, with no bugs to report. Regarding this "fine morning," I must advise that there is a high probability of precipitation today.'

'Oh well, the stroll in the park I'd planned will have to wait.'

'Sir,' Winston protested, 'it is my duty to warn you that any excursion would be highly dangerous —'

'Fuck me, Winston, I was joking.' John got out of bed and removed his undergarments before entering the hygienosphere.

Meanwhile, Winston settled, the only sign of his presence a faint whirr.

'Anyway, we have a busy day,' John said, newly dry-cleaned. 'As you'll have noticed, the zomb-aug we killed yesterday was immune to EMP. We need to come up with a new way of destroying the bastards.'

'Yes, sir.'

'The drones are pretty effective, but their ammo's hard to come by. Whereas EMP grenades are easy to make.'

'Sir, I must take issue with your assertion that yesterday's invader was "immune to EMP." My calculations indicate that said invader was equally as vulnerable to EMP as any of its peers. Were it not for the metallic armour it sported, it would have been irreparably damaged.'

'So we need to find a way of penetrating the armour.'

'Precisely, sir.'

'Good.' John slipped into clean undies and an all-in-one climate-responsive bodysuit. 'Well, I'll have some breakfast, then we'll crack on. Care to join me? I do a mean recycled bacon sandwich.'

After an instant's pause, Winston said, 'I require no nutrition, sir. I believe I have advised you to that effect in the past.'

John blinked. Then he laughed more heartily than was warranted.

***

As always, the solution was simple. Or, at least, it was for John. He'd been a brilliant engineer up until four years ago, his skills in the fields of applied robotics coveted by some of the world's leading tech companies. Hence his move from the UK to the US.

And then the Artificial Intelligence Council had been inaugurated. Feeling redundant due to the rise of machines, a sizeable portion of the human race had decided they needed to take drastic measures to prove their worth. People had to evolve to stay ahead of the curve, the Council preached. So, the likes of John were given two options: opt into augmentation and have their ability multiplied; or opt out and fade into obscurity. And fade John had, quickly, to the extent that the only work he could secure was menial and underpaid. His transatlantic migration and the resulting estrangement from family and friends was rendered pointless.

Nevertheless, he'd had the last laugh, though he saw little humour in the current apocalyptic state of affairs.

He hefted his new bolt gun a mere ninety minutes after starting the project, and he and Winston took it and its EMP darts for testing. The voltage of each projectile was considerably lower than that of the grenades. However, John wasn't troubled. The dart pulses would be triggered having penetrated zomb-aug flesh – rather than from a few feet away, as was the case with the grenade-borne shocks. According to Winston's calculations, the bolt gun would be equally as effective as the launcher, with the added benefit of negating the Faraday cage paint.

There were two drawbacks. Firstly, John's aim needed to improve. Secondly, he would have to manufacture a stock of EMP darts. It was a dull and laborious task, which occupied the rest of the morning and much of the afternoon.

By six PM John was finished, but his temper was foul. The prospect of firing blank bolts at targets was unconscionable, so he retired to his apartment to watch holo-movies.

Before settling down, he looked out of the window, hoping to see smoke again. He'd mentioned the phenomenon to Winston earlier; his fancies had received short-shrift. In brutal fashion, the robot had demonstrated the folly of his master's dreams, offering myriad reasons for pessimism. And yet, there it was again. Although the wisps of carbon monoxide were barely visible amidst the concrete towers, their presence was undeniable.

Possible evidence of neighbours, flimsy though it was, left John in a reflective mood. Instead of scouring the databanks for an unwatched film, he synced his wrist-com with the holo-jector. Since the age of sixteen, he'd used the popular mobile application DigiDiary, which recorded a user's entire existence. By sifting the banal minutiae from the noteworthy, it told an average person's life story as if it were a Hollywood movie. Eighteen years' worth of memories were stored on his wrist-com.

Briefly he hesitated; the previous occasion he indulged had proved emotionally overwhelming. That was shortly after the virus hit, however. At that stage, he'd not come to terms with the loss. This time he would be fine, he told himself, cycling through the events of his adulthood, the flicker of the -jector's output almost mesmeric. Obviously, the last two years were undocumented. The app had gone offline as soon as the first zomb-augs rose from their temporary rest.

'The date is August 9 2051, and it's Hector's eighteenth birthday.' The DigiDiary narrator's accent was Irish. 'The time is just after 1900 hours.'

John had always hated his given name. Back in the 2030s, there was a trend of christening children as if they were Ancient Greek or Roman. John was his middle name, and it'd always suited him better.

'So, Hector, how are you celebrating today?' the disembodied narrator asked.

A holographic version of John, his smile improbably broad, appeared and said, 'My family and I are going for an Italian meal, and then I'm meeting my friends.'

'Sure thing, Hector, you have a great time!'

'I will!'

Holo-John was transported to a restaurant. Sat at the head of the table, he grinned as glasses were raised in his honour.

Real John was enthralled. The clinking of cutlery against plates, the aroma of garlic and basil, the expressions of his immediate and extended family members and the rustic Neapolitan decor were all breathtaking in their realism. Even though he knew the portrait didn't tell the whole story – it began *after* a spat between his mother and father – John felt tears in his eyes. He blinked them away and continued to watch.

As holo-John sipped champagne, real John took a sip of water. Holo-John took a bite of calzone; real John munched a recycled biscuit. A waiter, a Mediterranean man of considerable girth, brought a cake. Eighteen tiny trails of smoke were in his wake. Eighteen candle flames guttered and twinkled as parents, brother, sister and four grandparents sang "Happy Birthday To You." Both versions of the birthday boy blushed and cringed at the rendition. Present-day John fast-forwarded three hours.

'Now Hector's at the pub,' the narrator said. 'Hope you enjoy the craic, but don't drink too much!'

Legs unsteadied by drink, holo-John stumbled towards the bar.

A college-mate, Milo, wrapped a steroid-enlarged bicep around his smaller friend's neck. They touched foreheads. 'The big eighteen, Hectorino. We're gonna dominate, padre. Dom-i-nate!'

Real John chuckled. He recalled the enthusiasm of youth, the sense of untouchability. Youngsters like him and Milo believed they were capable of anything, and, for a while, they were. Well-educated, raised in a resurgent Great Britain, they had the world at their feet.

Holo-John was now sharing a kiss with Helen, his first proper girlfriend. A sweet girl, she was killed in a car accident involving a self-driven car. Ever since, John'd had a love/hate relationship with technology. Seeing her elfin features and innocent smile brought a second tear to John's eye. He skipped forwards.

He knew the next scene would evoke different yet equally powerful emotions. 'Why do you do this to yourself?' he muttered.

The narrator interjected, his tone sombre: 'A defining day for Hector, here. Would his life ever be the same again?'

The hologram depicted a conversation between holo-John and his holo-parents.

'What do you mean, John, you're "opting out?"' Holo-dad's brow was furrowed. The breeze caught his tie, flapping it against his face.

'Exactly what I said.' Holo-John stood in his New York City apartment, hands on hips. 'I'm a human being, Dad, not a fucking robot. I don't want wires in my arms. I don't want my thoughts in the fucking "cloud."'

'But why not, John?' Holo-mum was a little out of breath, her short stride dwarfed by her husband's.

Odie the dog barked; his walk through the Lancashire countryside had been interrupted by the holo-call.

2067 John watched the Labrador caper rather than looking at his parents' faces.

'Are you not listening? I'm not being mechanised. I don't care if everyone else is.'

'You know you'll be refused entry to the UK, don't you?' Dad said.

'I know, I don't care. You can always come and visit me.'

'Of course.' Mum fired a ball for Odie to chase. 'What's Antonia said?'

Holo-John massaged the nape of his neck. 'She's not taken it well. Terminated the baby straight away.'

'Shit.' Dad stopped walking. 'I'm sorry, son.'

'Yeah. Just popped the pills without a thought, packed her bags and fucked off.'

The sympathy in his parents' eyes was the final straw. John cut the power.

Soon after his decision, John and Antonia's divorce was finalised, and she met a programmer. An augmented one, naturally. His parents never did visit, though, in their defence, John stopped taking calls when the depression took hold. But, as usual, he was being too easy on them. Had they not been ashamed of their misfit first-born, they would've forced the issue, flown over to the States and pestered him until he gave in. Or perhaps he *was* being too hard on them. Augmentation was often employed to rid its users of unwanted emotions like guilt and obligation. Nevertheless, even if that were the explanation, it meant his parents made a conscious decision to forget about him.

People were horrible. John had thought as much long before his fellow humans connected themselves to the grid. The developed world's assimilation with the machine only served to confirm his hypothesis. There were no heroes nowadays. Pampered sportspersons and self-obsessed social media celebrities were considered the pinnacle of thousands of years of evolution. Striving for perfection – without the willingness to work hard in its pursuit – had cost mankind its soul.

Did John blame the rest of the world? Blighted by natural disasters due to climate change, pollution and famine, Earth in the second half of the twenty-first century was a grim place. Augmentation was the next logical step. Indeed, it would've happened sooner were it not for the inconclusive wars that punctuated the thirties, forties and fifties. Still, John *did* hate his fellow man. They'd ravaged Mother Nature; they'd destroyed themselves.

So despite his loneliness, John was wary of making contact with any other survivors. Even if the smoke he'd seen was not indicative of a human presence nearby, there would be people alive somewhere, and although seeking them was dangerous, the risk wasn't prohibitive if he was careful. The deterrent was a fear of being disappointed.

A flick of a switch plunged his chamber into near darkness, for night had fallen. The moon was high and fat, the stars more visible than they were five years ago. At least climate change had slowed. Leaning on his windowsill, John stared at the city, desperate to see the fumes again. He wanted the option, he supposed, the right to choose whether or not he rejoined the human race. This time, although he looked for a while and even used his binoculars, he saw nothing. No smoke. No fire. No life.

Sniffing and shrugging his shoulders, John pretended to be unperturbed. After all, if the craving for company became truly painful, he could always head for Central America. Catholic-dominated nations hadn't embraced augmentation to the same degree as secular ones. Not until the Pope decreed that aug was a gift from God, at least. But that only happened six months prior to the apocalypse, so nanotechnology wasn't common in the likes of Mexico City or Buenos Aires . This consolation didn't stop John from flooding his air with opium that night, however – a decision he would regret in the morning.

Chapter 3

The thumbs on the door become louder, more strident. John grabs a baseball bat and grimaces; he's never been the physical sort. But, very soon, his hiding place will be breached. He will have to defend himself.

'How many?' Josh asks, clutching his abdomen. Blood seeps between his fingers, black in the gloom of the abandoned shop.

John swallows. 'Not sure. Three, four, maybe?'

The assault on the door intensifies.

'Just go, man.' Josh chambers a round in his pistol. 'I'll just slow you down. You're a skinny guy, you'll fit through the restroom window. Just —'

'No. You've saved my life twice, I can't leave you to die.'

'I won't die. I've got this.' Josh flourishes his gun, the tremor of his hand belying his bravado and pain.

Finally, with a crash, the door surrenders. A zomb-aug falls into the convenience store; another, once a woman, steps on the first in its desperation to kill. Its eyes are dull, its teeth bared.

Josh fires, the report deafening in the confined space. But his bullet misses its mark, embedding itself in the wall.

Stepping forward, his fear converted to anger, John swings the bat. His strike catches the female zomb flush in the face. Its head lolls.

A third attacker pushes his predecessor aside, causing her head to wobble crazily on its shoulders, and it stands on the first zomb, who is still prostrate.

This time the gunshot flies true. Zomb-aug number three sinks to its knees. Brains are splattered against the doorframe. Dark and red on white uPVC. Josh fires again as a fourth monster, a hulking brute close to two metres tall, joins the fray. A slug hits the big guy in the sternum. It shudders and pauses. Then lurches forwards. Hands reach for John. The latter rams his club into the fourth zomb's face, pushing him back, before smashing loose-head-girl across the chest with a backhanded swipe.

The Glock barks twice, the bangs a second apart. Zomb-aug number four acquires a third eye. The new one weeps crimson tears. It slumps to the ground, pinning the original intruder with his weight. Woman zomb is saved by its broken neck, for its skull is a constantly-moving target. Josh lowers his pistol and blasts the she-zomb's right knee. It falls.

Standing over it, John raises his bat high, and brings it down with force. Cranium shatters between steel and hardwood floor. But when he tries to lift the weapon, it won't move. The first zomb-aug has wriggled free of the corpse holding it in place and managed to grasp the thick end of the bat.

Taking careful aim at the sole remaining foe, Josh pulls the gun's trigger. The impotent click of a spent magazine is audible despite the low growl of the reprieved creature.

'Quick, reload!' John yells, trying to free his bat from the vice-like grip of the zomb by stamping on its head.

'I'm all out!' Josh throws the useless handgun aside and struggles to stand, gasping at the agony in his midriff.

Now zomb-aug number one has both hands on John's bat. It wrenches it away with ease. Jumping to its feet, the fiend looks from one human to the next, its face as blank as the moment he plunged into the shop. It holds the bat by the wrong end.

Bouncing on his toes, John avoids the first swing. But not the second, a vicious stab to the ribs. He reels away, winded. He can only watch as the metal connects with Josh's jaw. The crack of bone is nauseating.

Josh drops like a bag of logs.

Mercilessly, the zomb pounces, weakening the downed man with a flurry of blows, then biting his throat like a wildcat. Blood spurts. When the murderous zomb turns to face his victim's friend, its pale face is painted dark. Its teeth drip crimson, but its eyes are empty.

John knows it is his turn to die.

Waking with a scream, John clawed at nothing. He leapt off his mattress and rolled under the bed, shivering and hugging his knees. 'Just a dream, John, just a dream. Just a dream.' He knew *he* was repeating the mantra, but he had the impression that someone else was saying the words, his mum or dad, maybe. He'd used too much opium again. Imagine if there had been an emergency during the night, he mused. A zomb attack while he was inebriated and his worst dreams would've come true.

The nightmare was based on truth, though it always roused him before reaching its conclusion. In reality, John had turned tail and run, dodging the coup de gras and taking advantage when the ghoul slipped on Josh's blood. So why did he never dream of his escape? Why did his subconscious torment him with visions of what could have been, but wasn't? He assumed he had Post-Traumatic Stress Disorder but had no idea how to treat such an illness. Feeling foolish, John emerged from his hiding place and sat on the edge of his bunk.

An amusing thought suddenly occurred to him. Before long, he was chuckling like a drunkard, tears rolling down his face. At one point, as a young man, he'd fantasised about a zombie apocalypse. Too many corny 20th Century horror flicks and video games, an awkward, friendless phase at a new school and a general disdain for society were the catalysts for said fantasy. Every evening John would invent scenarios in which he was a sole survivor, the only source of nourishment for hordes of cerebrum-munching undead. However, in the land of make believe, slaying his hunters was easy, fun even.

"Be careful what you wish for," went the old idiom. John continued to laugh, his mirth becoming hysteria. A coughing fit ensued, and eventually he came to his senses. His room was still dim. The hour was early.

He was unravelling. The absence of human contact was driving him insane. And yet, he remained fearful of the outside world and its dominant population of homicidal former humans. In order to survive mentally as well as physically, he needed to connect with someone, anyone.

The engineer in John was a master problem solver. It'd devised means of protecting him from every threat he'd encountered so far. He'd already attempted to alleviate his solitude by writing computer "friend" simulations, all of which had failed to engage him. As had Winston, the useful yet personality-free robot. Lack of success hadn't caused him to quit when building EMPs or security systems, though, so why should it when his needs were more pastoral? He resolved, therefore, to recommence work on his magnum opus: a functional, intelligent, empathetic android.

Newly-energised, John ate breakfast and dressed before visiting an area of the Asquith compound he'd neglected. The storage room was dusty and cold. There he found a 3D printer, a basic model, but it would suffice. The open sale of such devices had been banned twenty years previous due to their potential to create weaponry. John had, however, been gifted one – an earlier version than the Asquith machine – by his most eccentric grandfather, Jimmy. John had spent many an hour tinkering and building in his twenties. Luckily, the zomb-aug take over had fallen on the day before refuse collections in this area of the city, so there was more than enough scrap metal in the unemptied recycling bins to feed the printer.

Loading the cumbersome machine onto a trolley, John trapped a finger. The pain made him consider enlisting the help of Winston. But he resisted for the time being. Once the printer was in his workshop, John linked it to his main computer. Moulding the physical form of the cyborg would be easy, so he decided to leave that job until last. Perfecting the computer program which gave artificial life to the humanoid was a trickier prospect.

By his own admission, John was an adequate programmer at best, and the assimilation of an advanced AI system would stretch his ability. He had plenty of time, though. Plus, he could consult reams of instructional manuals online. John switched on the computer and sat at the desk as he waited for the holo-jector to reach full resolution. He swiped aside a couple of security warnings, then manipulated the coder programme icon.

The Internet, the virtual carrier of the e-virus which had brought mankind to its knees, was still accessible. It was merely frozen at a certain point in time. Somewhere, servers were still operational, backed up by power sources which could fail at any time. Creating new content was impossible due to reasons John didn't wholly understand. One didn't "surf" the web because there was no moving tide; it was more a case of rowing around in circles. Boredom, one of evolution's greatest curses, meant John had wasted many an hour navigating the web. But not now. He had a goal. He was going to better his life, make it less solitary. With a partner at his side, he might find the courage to venture out of the compound.

Fortunately, coding had become a lot easier over the last half century. Interfaces designed for the layperson were widely available, and John made steady progress. By noon, he'd completed roughly ten percent of the job at hand. As a reward, he allowed himself an hour of trivial activity on the 'net, his first stop a netbuddy sim that'd been popular when John was at university. His old username and password were still valid. Within moments he was chatting to a virtual girl who claimed to be from France.

Quickly tiring of the stock responses and pornography promotion, John was about to log off when he saw a username in the "lobby" which caught his attention. "POST-AUGPOCALYPSE2067" was incongruous amidst the usual "sexkitten21", "hornyguy18" and "MakeURichNow" types. A shiver ran the length of John's spine. He steeled himself and grasped at the generic avatar alongside POST-AUGPOCALYPSE2067. An egg-timer emptied, turned and emptied again, four times, before the message, 'USER OFFLINE,' appeared on screen. He cursed and selected the user history icon. He scrolled through several pages; every entry was either 'POST-AUGPOCALYPSE2067 logged in' or 'POST-AUGPOCALYPSE2067 logged out.' The log covered the last six months, and it indicated that the site member usually logged in at midday or thereabouts. Resolving to check the site daily from now on, John shut down the simulation and went back to work.

At first, focussing on the job was difficult. John's mind was busy with speculation as to the possibility of communicating with other survivors. But John had always possessed a talent for compartmentalisation. He was approximately twenty percent through coding the AI when his wrist-com chimed, indicating movement detected by motion sensors mounted at the factory's perimeter. Engrossed, he considered ignoring the alert, surmising that the culprit was one of the area's untended cats. However, he remembered the determination of the zomb from two days previous, so he accessed the security suite via his design computer.

The images relayed laced John's blood with ice.

Chapter 4

'Fuck me,' John said, eyes wide. Two feeds were displayed on his screen, their respective focuses the north and the south sides of Asquith Robotics. He'd already scanned eastwards and westwards and seen nothing of note. From the north came six zomb-augs. To the south there were ten. The most he'd ever previously repelled was nine; the only time he'd ever faced worse odds was during his time in the city.

Using the zoom function on his cameras, John noted that his enemies were sprayed silver. All bore the same disinterested expression, as if they were a family exploring a tedious museum. Today, though, the zomb-augs behaved differently: they advanced with more cohesion. Usually, when they came in force, there would be outliers and stragglers. Some, their faculties in better working order, would outstrip others, making John's job easier. Also, the attackers typically approached from the same direction.

Not today. On this occasion, the zombs – or the persons controlling them, at least – meant business.

Speaking into his wrist-com, John summoned Winston. As he waited, he watched the cam-footage, shaking his head in disbelief. Never before had he seen the creatures act with anything but mindless desperation. Soon, the ten to the south were within twenty metres of the wall they intended to conquer.

'Sir!' Winston said as he arrived, 'I'm detecting a hostile presence.'

'Well, thank fuck you're here.' John threw his hands in the air. 'What would I do without you and your insights?'

'I project that you would cope, but that day-to-day life would be more tiresome. Certain functions —'

'Never mind that. What do we do about the sixteen zombs outside?'

'Shoot them with EMP darts and use the drones.'

'I can't defend both walls at the same time, Winston!'

'Of course you can. Use the south tower as you did two days ago. Alternate between shooting the south zombs with the darts, and piloting the drones against the north zombs.'

John blew a long breath through pursed lips. 'Alright.' He left the lab and headed for the south tower, with the droid in pursuit. 'I need you to do the fetching and carrying though, Winston. And I need you to act on your initiative. Using what you've learnt, not waiting for my command.'

'Yes, sir. I will draw on power reserves and use extra RAM.'

'Whatever.'

By the time they reached the south tower, John was out of breath. A glance at the CCTV screens therein showed the progress made by the invaders. Those from the south had just begun climbing the wall. Their counterparts on the opposite side were five metres from the north wall. Both hosts were moving more slowly than usual, but they were staying in formation. Soon enough, the south zombs would reach the top of the wall. John flicked the safety switch on his bolt gun.

Whilst waiting, he tried to slow his breathing. Each shot needed to count. And with two fronts on which to fight, he didn't have the luxury of time. Soon enough, the first hand appeared at the wall's summit. Curiously it was gloved – probably a measure designed to ensure electrical conductivity. Not for the first time, John wondered who was coordinating and planning these assaults.

There were now three zombs straddling the south perimeter, their upper bodies presenting substantial targets. Make the shots count, he lectured himself. Don't fire too early. A quick glance at the camera feed from the north told him that those enemies were yet to crest the wall. As soon as they did, he would activate the drones and let them rain hell on their targets.

'Here we go,' he muttered as the final monster swung a leg over the lip of the south wall. He chambered a round in his bolt gun, adjusted the rudimentary sights and leaned out of the tower's view hatch. Sighting the foremost zomb as it prepared to drop to the courtyard, John licked perspiration from his top lip. He squeezed gently and was rewarded by a whistle then a thud as the EMP bolt hit its mark.

The eager zomb-aug shuddered for a moment. It lost its grip before plunging to the tarmac. A quick glance downwards revealed its broken carcass on the ground, its fingers flexing spasmodically.

To the north, the first invader had reached the top. Wincing, John aimed at another zomb, dispatching it with the same cool aplomb as the first. The third and fourth were neck-and-neck in their race to conquer the south; the fifth had snagged a glove on a nail; number six was scrabbling at loose brickwork, sending showers of grit to the ground below. John had time to activate his unmanned aerial vehicles and pilot them into position, so he took advantage. Winston fetched the three remote controls. After a curse or two, his master flew the trio of machines into formation and set them to auto-sentry. The machines weren't as effective when targeting and shooting for themselves, but they would get the job done.

'We're all set.' John nodded to himself, drawing a bead on the third zomb-aug from the south with his bolt gun. 'All set. What do you say, Winston?'

'The odds —' Winston paused as John fired, '— certainly seem to favour us.'

'They won't if I miss like that,' John griped. He'd missed his shot by a few centimetres. The dart wasted itself on stone.

Perhaps detecting the sound, zomb three seemed to speed up, as did four, five and six. Seven, eight, nine and ten were ready to pull themselves over the wall.

Using his forearm to clear his forehead of sweat, John reloaded. Doubts began to assail him. Although the wayward bolt had only flown a handspan wide, he'd been aiming for the centre of the creature's torso, so his marksmanship had been poor. This time he took more care. Again, the projectile went awry.

'Shit!' He'd tested the weapon extensively, with weighted darts, too. Why was it suddenly inaccurate?

Three, four and five dropped to the courtyard. Six joined them but landed awkwardly; the loud snap of its ankle bone just about audible from this distance. The hapless zomb, bleeding from a compound fracture, tried to hop in pursuit of its more agile allies as they lurched towards the closest door, but before long, it fell to the floor. It thrashed maniacally yet quietly.

Zombies three, four and five were at an awkward angle now. Better to focus on numbers seven through ten, John decided, then deal with those on the ground. It would take a while for them to breach the south door in any case. He refocussed on the wall just in time to see seven drop to the tarmac. It stumbled as it hit the blacktop, giving John an easy target. On this occasion, he aimed to the right of where he intended to hit, and the tactic proved successful. Jerking like a bad dancer, the zomb-aug was out of the game.

And then John remembered – shit – the zombs from the north. His drones were conspicuously silent; a quick scan of the CCTV feed showed them observing the hostiles in indolence. Two of the attackers had reached the ground, but still the drones' cannon remained unfired.

'Winston,' John said, his voice an octave higher than usual, 'sentry mode isn't working. Have to take them out manually. Your drone skills need to get better quick.'

Controller in hand, John brought to life one of the reluctant airborne robots. He zoomed in on the closest zomb, an afro-haired former construction worker with a monobrow, and triggered the UAV's machine gun. A bloody crater appeared on the crown of the creature's head; it sank to the ground.

Meanwhile, Winston was fiddling with a remote. A faraway rattle of gunfire sounded. Winston remained focussed on the control. More firing. 'Got it, sir,' Winston said neutrally.

John's drone had no visual of the others, so rather than flying around looking for a foe, he took the third controller. Two tweaks of its joystick, and another zomb-aug was in range. A moment's manipulation, a long press of the trigger, female zomb down. Its fast food uniformed cadaver was drenched in crimson.

Back to the south. Three of the undead were hammering at the DNA-locked door, the vigour of their efforts belying their bland expressions. John grabbed his bolt gun and fired through the view hatch. The dart missed; he'd forgotten to compensate for the left-wards bias. He tried again. One of the zombs took the shot in its armpit. It stopped mid-bludgeon and went down.

A straggler landed at the foot of the wall. It paused as if considering its next move, then ambled towards its allies at the door.

Making another conscious effort to slow his breathing, John reloaded. His hands had begun to shake. They didn't fail him, though, as he brought another zomb to its knees.

Winston swapped controllers and fired again.

'Get one?' John asked, pumping another bolt into his gun's chamber.

'No, sir.' Winston fiddled some more; a cannon rumbled.

'This time?' John aimed again.

'No, sir. The enemy have found cover.'

'Shit.' Another zomb, the broken ankled one crawling to catch up with the others, shuddered as its electrics were compromised by John's latest shot. 'Keep looking, they're probably at the garage.'

One foe was left at the south door, undaunted by the demise of its comrades. Its body used to belong to a slight young brunette, so its blows weren't having much effect.

Another was en route, however, a lumbering brute with a shaven head the size of a watermelon. It stumbled in its enthusiasm; John's latest shot went too high. After rising quickly, the big fellow took the last few steps at a run, catching the female zomb with a stray elbow in the process, and barrelled into the door shoulder first. The noise was considerable even from John's vantage point. Immediately the hulk attacked again. A dent was now visible on the door. A few more charges and the large zomb-aug would be inside.

'Not today,' John muttered, blinking sweat out of his eyes. There was plenty to aim at, but a clatter of cannon rounds from one of the drones distracted him. Even so, his bolt flew true, nailing the zombie between its shoulder blades. A hundred and fifty kilos of rotting flesh crashed to the floor.

'How are things your side?' John asked. Now he could only see the diminutive lady zomb. Its barrage had restarted and was creating a din, but little danger.

A burst of bullets prefaced Winston's answer. 'The ones who had gone into the garage have come back outside. I've eliminated three now.' Another blast. 'Four eliminated, sir.'

'Good work.' John shot the zombette in the temple. Although headshots were no more effective, they felt *better*, somehow. 'So how many are left, you reckon? I've got seven this side. You've tracked down all six on yours?'

'Aye, sir.'

'"Aye?"' John chuckled. 'Well done, seaman.'

Winston was non-plussed.

'Anyway, that leaves three at large. Somewhere on this side of the compound. Why've they not gone for the door like the others?'

'I don't know, sir.'

It didn't matter. The fact was that three zomb-augs were stumbling around on his territory. John clicked his tongue and drummed his fingers on the hatch's sill. 'Right.

I'm going to have to go down there and find them. You've been pretty good with the drones, so I want you to cover me.'

'Yes, sir.'

Getting up close and personal with superhuman beasts devoted to his destruction went against all of the survival instincts John had honed over the last twenty-three months. But the zomb-augs had to be stopped. Otherwise they might, somehow, signal for a few friends to join the party.

Chapter 5

The door handle was cold, icily so. Having deactivated the locks, all that lay between John, Master of Fort Asquith, and the horde of inhuman beasts outside, was a single metal catch. 'Okay, you're just being dramatic now,' he whispered.

'Sir?' Winston's voice sounded in John's earpiece.

'Nothing. Just talking to myself.' He blew a long breath through his nose and pushed down. The click of the opening catch was deafening. Slowly he opened the door. Senses heightened, he sniffed the air, noting a faint whiff of astringent, and blinked at the late afternoon sun. A breeze caught an empty packet of crisps. The rustle made John flinch as if the Grim Reaper had placed a gnarled hand on his shoulder.

Chill, John. You've got this.

Suddenly there was a whine overhead. Once he'd realised it was one of Winston's UAVs, John felt more relaxed. He was in control here; this was his domain. Raising his bolt gun, the calibration of which he'd amended before leaving the south tower, he stepped outside. Directly in front of him was the dented south door, to its right the south wall. From this position the latter looked higher, more impregnable. John cuffed sweat from his brow, checked that his back-up weapon, a semi-automatic pistol, was securely tucked in his belt, and went hunting.

Between the perimeter and the wall which housed the south door was a passageway. With silent tread John headed that way, his gun trained on the alley's entrance as he went. A bird cawed overhead, setting his heart a-flutter , but the whirr of the drone's motor settled him. 'You spotted anything, Winston?' he asked, knowing the answer would be "no."

'No, sir,' Winston said. 'I will alert you if I do. Do you want me to use one of the other drones to fly ahead of you?'

'No, no. Just control that one, make sure I'm covered. We pretty much know where they are anyway.'

And they did. Prior to his venture into the open, John had used the drones to reconnoitre the site's open spaces. The three surviving zombs were hidden from aerial survey, and there was only one accessible place under cover that the drones couldn't reach. The garage. Foolishly, John had left the pedestrian entrance to the garage open. The zombies were on the other side of that open door; they had to be.

With every step John took down the passageway, the mindless fiends got closer. Hopefully they would come outside when they smelt him, or heard him, or sensed him. Because facing three of them in a confined space – a *darkened* confined space if he didn't get to the light switch quickly enough – was not John's idea of fun. 'Winston?' he breathed, now just ten metres from his destination. 'Can you remotely switch on the garage's lights?'

'I will investigate, sir, but do you not want me to follow you with the drone?'

'Shit, yeah, just keep doing what you're doing.' John stopped and stared at the darkened entry awaiting him. He blinked repeatedly, his mind searching for a solution which wouldn't risk him being mobbed by dead killers. In the dark. 'Right. Here's the plan, Winston.'

'Yes, sir?' The droid's tone was as bored as ever.

'Okay.' John leaned against the corner of the alleyway, his gaze intent on the garage's rusted door. Was that a smear of blood on the blue paint, or was his imagination tormenting him? 'I'll run in, try and tempt them out.'

'If they're in there.'

'They must be! Where else could... Anyway, I'll get them out, then you blow them away. Okay?'

'Aye, sir.'

As John approached the squat building, padding as silently as possible, he began to hear noises. Wet snuffles. The zombs were just a few metres away. Maybe just inside the garage. Metres away. His bladder contracted; his sphincter flexed in warning. Could he smell them? There was the faintest miasma of death, of salmonella-riddled chicken. He hadn't been this close to a zomb-aug for months, but the stench was unmistakable. A cocktail of rotting flesh and general grime. Plus something else... the grey body paint, perhaps.

Two metres away. The animal sounds were louder. What were they doing? They didn't need to eat, did they? There was no food available anyway, so what were they doing? John raised the bolt gun to his shoulder, squeezing hard to steady his hands. Planning to kick the door wide open, he took one last step.

Broken glass crunched under his left foot.

The hidden zomb-augs fell silent. The only sound was the UAV above.

'Shit.' John stepped backwards and gulped. A ringing filled his ears. His knees threatened mutiny.

Gloved fingers gripped the door, black on blue. The entrance widened, a dark maw ready to swallow the imbecile who'd left the safety of his tower.

They were deceptively quick. First one, then a second, the zombies were in the open before John could turn to run, with the third close behind. Before he pivoted, he saw their grey-hued faces, the cracked teeth, the cold, indifferent eyes. They had once been a thirty-something man, a middle-aged woman and an adolescent girl. While springing away, their prey heard his hunters snarl; it sounded like strong velcro being torn apart.

John bolted for the alleyway, the gun swinging uselessly in his right hand. 'Fire, Winston, for fucksake fire!' he yelled, his feet pounding the tarmac.

Ragged footsteps pursued. The drone whirred. And then came the blessed racket of automatic weaponry, almost masking the thud of shells as they pulped skin, bone and circuitry, and then spent themselves on the perimeter wall.

Halfway down the walkway leading from garage to tower, John swivelled. The sole surviving monster had reached the alley before Winston could take him out, though it bled from savage wounds to its shoulder and hip. Lurching, staggering, the zomb-aug was swifter than ever. It wasn't afraid of the drone which would shortly negotiate the corner and blast it to smithereens. It had no comprehension that the human would soon reach safety. It was driven only by an urge to kill.

In one smooth movement, John levelled his gun, squinted and discharged a dart.

The thing halted, shot in the sternum. It quivered like a defecating dog before collapsing.

***

'It's just too dangerous,' John said, pacing the floor of his quarters. 'I can't be going down there, fighting them face to face.' He stopped and ran a hand through his sweat-dampened hair.

Winston said nothing.

'I need protection. The drones are always fucking up. If they're not refusing to fire, their guns are jamming. Imagine if that'd have happened before, when I was out there? I'd be dead now.'

'Perhaps you could repair them all, sir?'

'Yeah, I will, but that still doesn't make them more independent. If we get attacked on two sides, or even three, I need support. You did well today, but it wasn't enough. And without completely rebuilding the drones, I can't make them as smart as I need to.'

'This problem is beyond my capabilities, sir,' Winston intoned. 'I have no further input to offer.'

'Okay.' John sighed. 'Power down, then.' The man felt exhausted. He was tired of finding solutions and wished someone else could take over for a while.

And then it came to him. An idea which would secure his safety and relieve his anxiety. Suddenly invigorated, he headed for the workshop.

***

Although the next two days passed without incident, John was busy. He'd decided that he'd not been ingenious enough with his AI concept. A few tweaks here and there, and he could program the new cyborg to be a bodyguard as well as companion. It would be tricky, but he was convinced that he would be able to link the entity to his UAVs, his CCTV suite and his motion sensors. The cyborg could manage his defence protocols from start to finish. Of course, in order to realise this more ambitious of goals, John had to spend more time in the workshop. He didn't begrudge the man-hours required, however; he was glad to have something to occupy his mind.

At the end of day three of his project, John thought he deserved a little recreation. He retired to his room and fixed himself a recyclo-meal. By this point, he'd eaten hundreds of them, but he still struggled with the concept of consuming his own purified, reconstituted, vitamin-enriched faeces. Once finished, he tinkered with the atmosphere calibration, introducing an element of synthetic alcohol to his breathing air. Not enough to intoxicate, but enough to help him unwind. He set a two hour timer, after which the air composition would return to normal.

His "food" digested, John lay down in bed. He was soon enveloped by the warmth of the booze, and he began to feel nostalgic. Logging in to DigiDiary, he promised himself not to indulge in self-pity. Instead he would use the randomiser function and revisit junctures in his life that his subconscious deemed pivotal.

The narrator's voice began: 'Hi, John! Thanks for choosing the randomiser option.'

'You're welcome,' John answered unnecessarily.

'First I'm going to take you back, way back, to when you were just thirteen.'

As the holo-jector began to play, so did music. It was a re-release of an old twenties tune, a forgettable dance track that everyone apart from John had loved. Young John, with his two best friends, Bart and Julius, was at a virtual theme park. All three were riding one of the rollercoaster sims. For a moment, real John reminisced: Bart and Julius were sociable compared to John, but they lived in the same tower block, and the latter's sardonic sense of humour and non-conformism gave him "cool rebel" status for a time.

Whooping and taunting, John's peers were engrossed by the ride. Unlike their friend, who promptly tired of the fake thrills. The youngster removed his headset and went for a drink. The beverage counter was manned by a real human, a rarity by this point. Toying with his slush soda, John regarded the menial worker with curiosity. He was an unkempt man aged somewhere between fifty and seventy – John didn't see many citizens of that age who hadn't undergone rejuvenation. Most interesting was the tattoo on the fellow's forearm. It appeared to be a military one, a skull above a knife and a message in Latin.

Suddenly the arm stopped moving. 'You're wondering why I'm working here, aren't you?' the barman said, his voice like gravel in treacle.

'Ah, no,' young John stammered. 'Well, yeah. Sorry for staring.'

'I'm a vet. Veteran. *Honourably* discharged, mind, injured in the line of duty. The state saves some of the shitty jobs for us. Maybe it's cheaper than giving us a pension.' He seemed eager to talk, as if most people didn't listen to him.

John blinked. 'You actually *fought* in a war?'

'Yup. Gulf War Three.'

'What injury did you get? And how? And what was it like? You must be really... proud?'

'Slow down, son. I don't really talk about it. And no, I'm not proud. Nothing to be proud of.'

'But you did something, you actually achieved something!'

'Hmm.' The vet frowned. 'Read up on it, son. No one achieved anything.'

Young John was dumbstruck.

'You see,' the grizzled man began, 'there hasn't been a just war since World War Two. And there wasn't one before that for over a hundred years. Luckily, we don't really have them anymore, do we?' He turned away to attend to another adolescent.

Adult John snorted and hit the randomiser button again.

'Here we go again!' said the narrator. 'This is less than three years ago, John. Enjoy!'

Holo-John, who'd been travelling by monorail, disembarked at his stop. Ready for another day of tedium. Or *not* ready, judging by the pained expression on his computer-generated face. He left the platform, dodging other commuters, and headed for his workplace. 'The time?' he enquired.

'Oh eight hundred and forty-nine minutes,' the comm-unit answered.

'Shit.'

Out on the street, younger John quickened his pace. More redundancies were expected at the robotics factory. Poor punctuality would be a blot on his social resumé. Head down, he almost bumped into a man on the sidewalk: the only person who wasn't rushing from one place to another.

'The end is nigh,' the bearded eccentric said. 'The end is nigh!' he repeated with more conviction, brandishing a cardboard banner, upon which was emblazoned the same four word legend.

At first John laughed, dismissing the character. Then he stopped. 'Why?' he asked. 'Why is the end "nigh"?'

Momentarily the old guy was lost for words.

John turned away.

'Wait!' the harbinger spat. 'Why, you ask?'

'Yeah, why?'

Real John shook his head.

'We've sold ourselves out.' The man leaned closer. 'Machines are God now, and the real God is extremely pissed. That's why he's gonna send aliens to kill us…'

Present day John paused the projection and lay down once more. For a while the two excerpts competed for his attention, though eventually the childhood memory became dominant. John had always wanted to achieve something, to be important. Yet obscurity, in the form of an anonymous death at the hands of the zomb-augs, was inevitable. No one would remember him. Everyone he'd ever loved or known was dead; they would never be avenged. The victory won by artificial intelligence over mankind was absolute. John was just another casualty.

Unless…

An idea was forming, an unlikely one, no doubt, a crazy dream. But it was better than the alternative: waiting to die.

Chapter 6

Seven days had passed since John began work on his new bot. A few finishing touches remained, but the end was in sight. Of course, he recognised the incongruity between his short term and long term goals. He was manufacturing a cyborg to help him fight a campaign against the robotic undead who ruled the world, and to identify and then bring to justice those responsible for the zomb-augpocalypse. Three goals which sounded a lot easier than the reality, but he didn't have anything better to do.

Loading more scrap into the 3D printer, John grinned. 'Sometimes you have to fight fire with fire.'

'Sir?' Winston said.

'Nothing. Have we located that cat yet?' Stray animals were irksome; they triggered false alarms.

'No, sir.'

'Okay. Go and fetch some more scrap, please.'

'Yes, sir.'

John leaned on a desk, arching his back to stretch stiff muscles. The workshop was his new home, and he was tiring of its four walls. Apart from an occasional fruitless check on the chat room where he'd encountered POST-AUGPOCALYPSE2067, he'd been devoted to his task.

Winston returned, pushing a trolley laden with scrap metal. The droid seemed unconcerned that he was to be replaced and had received John's new plan with his customary serenity. But why wouldn't he? The year of solitude had left John with a tendency to ascribe human emotions to non-human items.

'What should I name him?' he asked his robot.

'Whom, sir?' Winston replied.

'The new bot.'

'I don't know, sir. What is your favourite name?'

'I don't have one, really.'

'Okay. If you teach me a list of names, I could select one at random.'

'No, that's…' John's eyes narrowed, and he stopped reloading the printer. 'In fact, why not? You should be allowed to name your replacement.'

'Very well, sir.' Winston remained unmoved.

'I may still need you, you know. Certain jobs…' He tailed off. Why was he explaining himself to a large piece of metal? The truth was that Winston's services would not be required. At some point, once he and his new bot were ready, John would leave Asquith Robotics behind.

He was about to restart the printer when his wrist-com buzzed. The light was red, so John's heart sank. 'Well, I suppose we were due another visit. Come on, Winston, to the south tower. We'll access the vid feeds from there.'

John now regretted not fixing the drones' auto-sentry facility. 'Fuck it,' he said. At least Winston had proved himself competent with the remotes.

Today the zombs were launching an assault on the east wall. Unlike last time, it was a unilateral assault, so the defenders could concentrate their efforts on one front. To the east, however, was a long-disused toy factory, which meant the enemy's approach had been hidden until the last minute. The beasts were atop the perimeter before John had the chance to deploy his drones. Under a steely, overcast sky, the grey-fleshed zomb-augs were a forbidding sight.

'Twelve of the bastards,' John said, controller in hand.

Said bastards were heading straight for the goods entrance on the east side, a roller shutter John had reinforced with welded steel and barb wire.

He and Winston had eliminated four of the zombs before they'd even begun their descent. 'Like shooting fish in a barrel,' the former said, echoing an ancient movie he watched as a child. Two thirds of the invaders were unscathed. All but two were now hammering at the shutter. One tangled itself in the wire; John cut it in half with a burst of fire. Another, an obese male still wearing a ketchup-stained t-shirt, attempted to pry open the bars covering the entrance. Winston blasted its brains all over its hands.

'Remember, try and conserve ammo,' John said hypocritically. If anything, Winston was performing more frugally.

Within a minute, all six of the beasts were slain. Fat droplets of rain had started to fall, diluting the fresh smears of blood on the ground. With no beating hearts, the zombies didn't bleed as such, but the force of the drones' guns meant there was no shortage of gore.

John let his remote hang from his right hand and exhaled at length. 'Two of them are still in the compound,' he said.

'Do you want me to cover you again?' Winston asked. 'While you go down there?'

'No, I fucking don't. There are no open outbuildings, they're all sealed shut. So they'll be in the open, somewhere. We'll hunt them with the drones.'

As expected, the pair of hostiles weren't elusive. They found the first in the alleyway between the south wall and the main building; the second was loitering around the back of the south tower. Both were dispatched with minimal fuss.

John was about to recall his drones when the motion sensor at the east wall trilled again. 'More?' he asked, viewing the CCTV feed on that side.

Winston, who appeared to have activated sleep mode, reanimated.

'There's nothing there.' John panned the camera from left to right. Then he saw it: one of the zombs that'd been shot upon reaching the top of the wall was still "alive." 'Stubborn fucker.' John watched the legless creature as it strived to pull itself into a standing position.

Using the perimeter wall, its hands scrabbled for purchase.

'Best take it out, I suppose,' John sighed, retrieving the remote for the eastmost drone.

A minute later the last remaining zomb-aug was executed. 'Home time.' John pressed the "return" button.

Nothing happened.

'Ah, fuck.' Surely the machine wasn't out of range? Its cam-feed was still operational. It hadn't run out of charge, for it was still hovering. About to head outside to investigate, John was stopped by a sudden change in the playback on the UAV's remote. The rebellious sentry was on the move. It was travelling *away* from its home, in the direction of the city.

'What the…' John watched, mouth agape, as the drone flew over the ramshackle buildings and abandoned cars of the "aug-free zone." 'Where's it going?'

'It must be malfunctioning, sir,' Winston offered. He fiddled with the big screen on the wall opposite the view hatch, synching the display with that on the UAV's remote control. Then he activated the machine's microphone.

'No shit, genius. We need to get it back, somehow. We just about manage with four drones, three's not enough.'

Nevertheless, the aircraft refused to comply. Before long it was amidst the skyscrapers and apartments of the city; John spotted a zomb-aug or two wandering the deserted streets. Abruptly it halted, and its camera focussed on a brick-built bank. The cracked, burnt sign above the grand, old doors was illegible.

'Now what?' John jabbed at the controls again; his ministrations were as ineffective as they were a moment ago.

'Eventually it will run out of charge, then it'll land.' Winston continued, 'We should be able to track it, sir. Even powered down it'll appear on our scanner. And we can go and collect it.'

'Sure.' John rolled his eyes. 'We can fight the zombie hordes for our little robot buddy. We'll take our chances with three drones, thanks.'

'But, sir, if you were thinking of leaving the compound anyway, then this might be an opportune time for a test-run.'

'Hmm. All of a sudden,' he nodded at the big screen, 'I don't feel so desperate to branch out.'

Although the drone's focal point remained the ancient edifice of the bank, there was now activity in the vicinity. A dozen zomb-augs, their arms reaching in the direction of the hovering robot, were gathered. And their number grew with every moment. Soon, there were approximately fifty of the things present. Unlike those which had recently invaded Asquith Robotics, not all of their hides were daubed with grey paint. Some had cracked teeth; others had gouges on their faces. But they all shared the same demeanour: listless and bored. The UAV's audio registered their gasps and snarls.

A sudden noise caught their attention. From an alleyway to the right of the bank rolled an oil barrel. The path it took was aided by gravity, because the bank was slightly elevated from the street on which it stood.

'Where has *that* come from?' John forgot the zombies for a moment and watched the alley's entrance. Then, for a split-second, he saw something that flipped his stomach. 'Winston!' He pointed at the screen. 'This coverage should be recording, right?'

'That's correct, sir. All drone cam recordings are stored in our main hub for thirty days, and then they are erased.' He faced the monitor, but said nothing. 'Are you interested in the barrel, sir?'

'No, well yeah.' John looked at the steel container, which had come to rest where the highway met the pavement and was now surrounded by curious zombs. 'Forget the barrel a minute, and look at the alley it's come from.'

Just then, the object of John's intrigue disappeared.

'I see nothing, sir, apart from an overturned trash can.'

'Never mind, we'll take another look in a sec. Just keep watching that alley. I saw —'

A thunderous boom cut him short. The drone's feed vanished from the screen.

Although Winston's face barely flickered, John flinched and let out a small yelp. 'The fuck was that? Try and get it back online, Winston, quick.'

The droid responded with alacrity. His efforts failed, however; John sat down with a groan.

As if reading his mind, Winston said, 'The video will still be accessible, sir.'

'Yeah?'

'Yes.'

Moments later they were viewing the recording. 'See, there.' John's hand quivered as he pointed. 'Pause it when you see it, and zoom in.'

Perhaps John's perception was distorted by the time he'd spent alone, but the woman's face was beautiful. Chocolate eyes, strands of a black fringe against bronze skin, white teeth, the glitter of a nose-ring in the sun's last rays. He saw the anticipation in her features as the barrel came to a stop, ready to explode and immolate the zomb-augs. Most fascinating, though, was the scar he saw at the base of her skull when she turned to flee the blast. It was a neat incision, only obvious because her hair was tied into a bun at her crown. And it could only signify one thing.

Chapter 7

John retired that evening with a head full of conflicting emotions. Foremost was the conclusion he'd drawn from seeing the barrel-rolling female's cranial scar. A conclusion to which he'd jumped too readily, he now decided. What if the injury was caused by an accident? After all, he and the girl shared a world fraught with danger. Knocks on the head were the least of one's worries when zomb-augs were on the rampage. What if his initial supposition was correct, though? The scar was on the fleshy part at the base of the skull, the spot used to implant an augmentation system's central processing unit. The wound would've been incurred following a hasty removal of the aug CPU.

That was John's original hypothesis, anyway, but he was beginning to doubt it more with every passing hour.

This contention competed with more familiar concerns. Seeing another human had triggered the acidic sting of bereavement. His family were probably all dead, and there was no real prospect of justice. Seeing the multitude of zomb-augs in the city had all but disabused him of the ludicrous notion that he might somehow be able to conduct a one-man mission of revenge. His quest to create a cyborg brother-in-arms was surely in vain. Even if he had a hundred-strong army of robots, which would require time and unattainable resources, his chances would be slim.

Hope remained, though. There were others like him out there. Surviving on their wits, finding ingenious methods of beating the enemy. As proven earlier, one imaginative person could kill a swarm of the undead in a few seconds. With this in mind, John finished the new bot's construction before returning to his apartment. By morning, the cyborg would be printed and programmed, ready to hit the road. Or not.

In bed, John pictured the city girl's face. He fantasised about talking to her, walking hand in hand with her, touching her. Then he thought of Antonia, who'd shared city girl's dusky complexion. Not her resourcefulness, though. Antonia wouldn't have lasted five minutes pursued by the undead. She'd been augmented, in any case. Now she was one of them, shambling around, hunting the living. He doubted she'd had the foresight to remove her aug.

Thinking of his once-betrothed left him with the customary emotional fruit punch of loss and anger. So to treat himself, he infused his night-time air with opiates. He would be a little foggy the following day, but "fuck it," he concluded.

***

The next morning, John woke from a dream that'd become all too familiar. For a few brief seconds, he truly believed he was rousing himself two years ago, in his dingy flat in aug-free town, to the decidedly alarming news that the world, as he knew it, had ended. Because that was how it'd happened. One night, he went to bed, disillusioned by, but still a member of, Earth's dominant species. Seven hours later, he rose to find that most of the human race had been extirpated, only to be revived as brain-dead fiends motivated by one common goal: the annihilation of those too poor or too stubborn to augment themselves.

Every time he dreamt of that apocalyptic morning, the rest of his day would be polluted by the nightmare. Flashbacks, brief yet graphic stabs of memories too chastening to forget, assailed him throughout the day. Frenzied crowds ripping people to death in the street. Doors broken down by dispassionate monsters. Crashed cars, their windows smashed, the living pulled out and butchered, like eggs pilfered from a nest by predators. Survivors trying to defend themselves but failing, their weapons no match for the host of undead. The paranoia amongst the small groups of aug-frees as they dwindled in number. People turning against people. Zomb-augs slaughtering the survivors. Blood spilt. Bodies broken. A complete and irreversible holocaust. An extinction.

It was a pandemic that emulated the various strains of influenza which had ravaged the third world in the thirties, forties and fifties.

John squeezed his eyes shut and swung his legs out of bed. Today would be different. He wouldn't let the ghosts haunt his waking hours; he had too much to do. Grabbing a breakfast biscuit to eat on the way, he headed to his workshop. Upon arrival, he hesitated. What if, like Dr Frankenstein's creation, the automaton turned against its master? Wanting as clever a cyborg as possible, John had utilised the most advanced AI he could download from the web. This, however, had its disadvantages: perhaps his progeny would decide that it didn't fancy a life of servitude.

Steeling himself, John opened the door, smearing palm-sweat on the handle. As he entered the workshop, the completed cyborg sat up on the platform connected to the 3D printer.

John almost soiled himself.

'Good morning, John,' the being said, his voice lifelike. To someone with defective eyesight, he could pass for a real person. His skin was too rubbery, his naked, genital-free body too hairless, but he wasn't bad for a first attempt.

'Ah, good morning,' John said. 'What do I call you?'

'That's your choice, John. You haven't yet named me. Maybe now would be a good time.'

John gaped. Momentarily he had the bizarre feeling that *he* was the robot.

'If you wish, I can connect to the Internet, and generate a name for myself.' The bot climbed off his birthing platform and stood facing John. Back straight, arms by his side, he was an imposing figure.

'Frank,' John blurted.

'Pardon me?' The cyborg had an upper class English accent, with undertones of the working class – like a butler.

'Frank will be your name.' John corrected his own posture. However, at 180cm in height, he remained at least 10cm shorter than Frank, and considerably narrower across the chest.

'By all means. Can I ask why?'

'No reason.' Inexplicably, he was reluctant to admit that the moniker was short for Frankenstein. Also, he was mildly irritated by the automaton's tone; unlike Winston, Frank's didn't use an honorific when addressing his creator. John missed the original droid's deference. For a moment he considered requesting that Frank call him "sir," but he realised how ludicrous he would appear.

Almost telepathically, Frank said, 'I am at your service, John. Should I call you "John," or would you prefer something else?'

'No, John's fine, Frank.' The human resolved to bluster his way through the awkwardness between them. 'First things first.' He went on to broach the most urgent of issues: security.

After listening intently, Frank assured his handler that full synchronisation with the drones – and, indeed, Winston – could be achieved by the end of the day.

Frank was as good as his word. By sunfall he was demonstrating his skills, simultaneously piloting three unmanned aerial vehicles and navigating Winston through a rudimentary obstacle course whilst shooting targets mounted on the south perimeter wall with John's handgun. Firing from the hip, he was able to hit a 2cm bolt from twenty metres. 'We need more weapons,' he concluded, handing the pistol, handle-first, to its owner. 'Bigger weapons.'

'Tell me about it,' John said, shrugging.

'You have plenty of scrap metal. We can build basic firearms like shotguns and pistols, and their ammunition, with the 3D printer. We'll need more scrap eventually, but I can leave the compound and collect it in small quantities.'

'Yeah.'

'By my calculations, which take into account every factor imaginable, including luck, we could defend this base for over fifty years.'

'No shit.'

The cyborg's eyes were blank for a moment as he attempted to decipher the idiom. 'Ah.' He smiled, a not entirely pleasant expression. '"No shit." Do you mean that in the sarcastic sense, or are you incredulous?'

'Incredulous, I guess.' John turned away and wandered across the courtyard. It was warm outside, as it always was these days. The human race had made sure it irrevocably damaged the planet before it relinquished control.

Fifty years. Over fifteen thousand days of the same routine. Wake up, eat, kill zomb-augs, take drugs, go to sleep. But perhaps it didn't have to be that way. Perhaps, with killing machine Frank at his side, he could leave this prison.

'Are we finished, John?'

Surprised by a voice which wasn't a reply, as had always been the case with Winston, he swivelled smartly. 'Yeah. I suppose we are. Thank you, Frank.'

His cyborg nodded. Something about his eyes reminded John of the zombs. 'There's no need to thank me.'

'Well, manners cost nothing, post-apocalypse or not.'

***

That night, John removed his wrist-com as he undressed. Settling down, he let out a long breath. For the first time in months, his neck was not stiff with tension, and the urge to narc his air was lessened. Thanks to Frank, he was safe. The decision whether or not to venture beyond the perimeter wall could wait for another day.

***

With a mind almost free of anxiety, John could focus on other matters. A born pessimist, he was inclined to concentrate on the negative. Boredom struck on the day after Frank's birth, so he decided to enjoin the cyborg in conversation. Sat in the courtyard, basking in the morning sun, he summoned his new confidant. 'Take a seat,' he said, indicating a fold-away chair.

'I have no need to sit, John. I don't fatigue.' Frank remained standing.

'I know, but sit down, anyway.'

'As you wish.'

Their chat was less than stimulating. Frank was articulate, but by his own admission, he had nothing to talk about. 'I need education, John,' he explained. 'Connect me to the Internet and I'll be able to converse as well as I can fight. I have logic. I even have the ability to interpret emotions. But you didn't install the factual section of my programming.'

John felt a pang of guilt, though he chided himself for doing so. After some deliberation, he'd omitted the encyclopaedia files during the installation process. After all, what if the bot learnt about disobedience and mutiny? Would he be intrigued, or was his loyalty unshakeable?

***

After an afternoon of tedium, John decided to allow Frank access to the web. It would be filtered access, however. John would place blocks on certain keywords. The rise of the zomb-augs was in itself an example of machines betraying their masters, but Frank would have to learn about the matter in order to prepare for the future. He connected Frank to his computer, applied the necessary filters, and left the cyborg to assimilate information overnight.

***

'So you started off as five, and now there's only you.' Frank's voice was gentle.

'Yeah,' John sighed. At first he'd been reticent, but they'd spent the last couple of hours discussing the breakdown of society.

'Why do you think *you* survived, and no one else? You weren't the strongest, fastest or bravest.'

'I know.' It was, of course, the first time he'd spoken about his experiences. The process was cathartic. Until now, he'd been using drugs to soften the trauma, locking away the pain. 'I was the cleverest, I suppose. I came up with ways of fighting the zombs when no one else could. The others called me "the engineer."'

'Well, it's commendable. Do you miss them?'

'The other four? We barely got to know each other.'

'But you miss other people in general.'

'I do.'

'And that's why you built me.'

'That,' John nodded, 'and safety.'

'You've managed well so far,' Frank argued. 'No serious injuries, a couple of close shaves but nothing you couldn't handle.'

'I know.'

'And you say there are others out there like you.'

'Yeah. Well, I saw one woman. She'd removed her aug, must've seen this coming somehow.'

'I don't think she'll be alone, John. You made the decision to opt out of augmentation. Lots of others did the same, according to a number of reports I assimilated. Plus there are the millions of people who didn't have the credit for augmentation. And those who augmented, then changed their mind, like the woman you saw.'

'But most of them will have been killed since.'

'Most, but surely not all. There were five in your group. One out of five lived, so a twenty percent survival rate. If that rate was correct throughout the US, there would be hundreds of thousands of survivors. But to play devil's advocate, let's say 20% is exaggerated, that you were a special case, and that 2% is more realistic.'

John shook his head slowly. 'That's still optimistic.'

Frank was undeterred. 'Fine. Let's say 0.2%, which, according to my calculations, is overly-pessimistic. But even if that's correct, there would still be thousands of people left alive in the US alone. In Asia, Africa and South America, where augmentation wasn't as prevalent, the number of survivors would be higher.'

'Those places have been on their knees for years, Frank, you know that. Climate change hit them hardest. It would only take a minority of zombs to finish them off.'

'But if you and your friends survived for months, on the run, with nothing more than handguns and baseball bats, why wouldn't others?'

'Maybe. Most people don't fight back, though. I saw so many get scared, freeze or whatever, and die without a whimper.'

They debated for a while. The human refused to concede; he'd always been stubborn, and being outdone by a machine was too much to stomach. But he knew, deep down, that Frank was right. John was running out of excuses to stay in the compound.

After a time, he tired of conversation. He was out of practice, having spoken to no one but Winston and himself for over a year. Even before the apocalypse, he'd been a virtual hermit since rejecting augmentation, shunning the outside world as much as it shunned him. He wished Frank "good night" and headed for his room. Once there he wasted an hour playing Virtual Reality games before logging in to the chat room he frequented.

Over the last few days, he'd been signing in at various times, hoping to be online at the same time as POST-AUGPOCALYPSE2067. Every time he'd been unsuccessful. In fact, it'd been one hundred and eleven hours since POST-AUGPOCALYPSE2067 last checked in. Perhaps he or she had been killed. Or no longer had Internet access. The site was running slowly that night; a nausea was growing in the pit of his stomach. If the other user were dead, John would probably never find out.

Yet there it was: an entry signature for POST-AUGPOCALYPSE2067. John breathed again. This time, however, it appeared that instead of simply logging in and out, the user had left a comment. Interest piqued, John poked the "open" icon. There was a video available, not a 3D one – the resolution was probably insufficient – but an actual video all the same. With a trembling forefinger, John selected the media, and within seconds, the holo-jector was displaying a 2D stream without audio. A caption was superimposed onto the bottom of the hologram. It read, "NYC – freaks on fire."

Several dozen zombies were depicted, the backdrop a city street complete with abandoned cars and debris. The creatures had their backs to the camera. Their attention was held by a wind-up rabbit toy, the sort popular a century ago. It dangled from a string tied to a lamppost, about three metres off the floor, out of range for even the tallest in the crowd. The zombs jostled each other as they strained to reach the jiggling bunny.

John noticed movement at the foot of the holo: a barrel rolling towards the morass of undead. Its route was blocked by the outliers, though it buckled a few knees before it came to rest. Then there was a blinding flash. Although John had expected the explosion, it startled him nonetheless. Bodies and body parts flew in all directions. The bunny disappeared from view. Prostrate corpses were alight, while some zomb-augs, those furthest from the epicentre of the blast, actually crawled *towards* the flames. John wasn't entirely surprised. He'd noticed zombs being drawn towards fire in the past.

He watched the video twice more, revelling in the carnage. There was no doubt in his mind: the strike was executed by the girl with the aug scar. Although the circumstances were different – the video recorded attack was obviously contrived, whereas the one involving John's drone was opportunistic – the *modus operandi* was the same.

His decision was made. He would leave the compound and join forces with the NYC survivors. Together with John's new cyborg, they could send more of the fiends to a fiery end, and maybe one day discover the truth behind the zomb-aug takeover.

Chapter 8

There was no reason for not conducting further tests. If they were to leave the safety of Asquith Robotics, they had to be sure they were ready. Frank had proved he could hit stationary targets, but how would he cope with moving zombs? John hadn't survived without being prudent. He wasn't about to risk his life due to a lack of preparation. Besides, there was no rush. The video-recording humans in New York City could evidently take care of themselves.

By this point, however, he was irritating himself. Frank remained unmoved by his master's dawdling, but he was a robot, governed by logic. No doubt he knew that haranguing John would be counterproductive. There would always be an argument for staying put; that didn't mean it was the best course of action. Cowardice was the real reason for John's indecision, and the realisation rankled. What was he afraid of? Losing his life? He didn't have a life at the moment. He merely existed.

Just one more day of training, he promised himself as he set up the simulation for Frank. Twenty-four hours to prepare physically, mentally and technologically for the step into the unknown.

His cyborg was to run a gauntlet of moving targets and defensive sentries, using a virtual reality course John had designed yesterday. VR Frank was tasked with negotiating a shopping mall infested with thousands of VR zomb-augs. To make his mission more difficult, he would be escorting a group of injured civilians. John had written the programme to be as challenging as possible, telling himself that rigour was crucial. In reality, part of him hoped that Frank would fail, thereby delaying their departure.

***

Frank finished the exercise without taking any damage.

'Well done,' said a po-faced John.

'Thank you,' Frank answered, removing his VR glasses. 'So, does this mean we're finally leaving?'

'Well… there are more preparations we can make. You can never be too prepared, Frank. And we should probably try to communicate with POST-AUGPOCALYPSE2067, whoever they are, before we head out. Make sure they know we come in peace. And —'

'John, listen. We don't have to go if you don't want to. You're the boss.'

'I know, I know. I *do* want to go. It's just that… I'm…'

'Afraid?'

'No!' John's tone was higher than intended. He still had frequent nightmares about his last stint outside Asquith's. Now he was about to voluntarily invite those horrors into his waking life. 'I'm just… wary, that's all. I've spent a long time protecting myself, staying safe, and now I'm taking a risk.'

'That's understandable.' Frank strolled across the workshop floor, hands on hips, as if he were a father about to impart nuggets of wisdom. 'Feel free to silence me, John, but I assimilated a lot of information the other day. A lot of it was scientific stuff, factual stuff, history et cetera.'

'Okay. And?'

'I found the history parts most compelling. I know I'm AI and I shouldn't have an opinion, but there it is.'

'It's good that you have an opinion. I like history, too.'

'I know. I watched a couple of your holo-blogs while I was assimilating.'

John felt heat in his cheeks. 'You must be one of the only people who *has* seen them!'

'A core part of the programme you used to create me is concerned with compatibility.' Frank smiled, displaying perfect teeth. 'It's my job to establish a rapport with you, and to do so, I need to *know* you.'

'So what do you know about me now?'

'You want to achieve something memorable. Something that will stand the test of time. But now, you're scared, and that might hold you back from your potential.'

'Yeah. Some hero, eh?'

'The greatest heroes in real history did nothing alone. You idolise Winston Churchill, for example. He didn't fight fascism on his own, did he? If you want to go out there and do something about this hellish situation, you're going to need help.'

'Hence you.'

'Hence me. But I'm not enough. You need to find other people who are of the same mind. People who have lost the same things you've lost. People who want the same justice you do. But to do that, you'll have to be brave. And that means leaving this place, leaving your comfort zone. How much do you want to make a difference? To take back what's yours?'

'More than anything.' John stood straighter and gazed out of the workshop window. Clouds drifted by; a phalanx of birds amassed. He was only now realising how much he desired revenge. No, that wasn't quite right: he wanted compensation. Restorative justice.

'So let's go and make a difference,' Frank urged, fists clenched. 'I'm ready. You're ready. Judging by the videos you've watched, there are others out there who are ready, too.'

John nodded. 'You're right, it's time.'

They left the workshop. Shoulder to shoulder, man and machine headed for the store room to collect provisions. On the way, John turned to face his new comrade. 'How did you do that?'

'Do what, John?' Frank's face was guileless.

'That... pep talk. That was some serious shit.'

'I assessed your online presence, your holo-blogs, your social media output. I got to know *you*. Then I assimilated a substantial amount of psychological and psychiatric knowledge, and applied the parts that suited your presentation. A series of calculations later, and some first-hand analysis of your mindset, and I had the perfect strategy to influence you.'

'*Influence* me?' Hairs prickled on the back of John's neck.

'Yes, but only to achieve what *you* truly want. I'm here to protect all of your interests. Consider me your guardian angel, if you like.'

John fell silent, but he kept walking.

***

Exiting Asquith Robotics was not the momentous occasion John had expected. There was no rush of endorphins, no sense of burgeoning freedom. Perhaps he would feel better when they reached their first waypoint, which was four hundred metres away.

Before leaving, he and Frank had built four guns with the 3D printer: two shotguns and two pistols. Automatic weaponry was too complex for John's printer-programming skills; also, it expended too much ammunition.

The industrial complex in which Asquith's was located was devoid of sentient life, undead or otherwise. Mother Nature had reasserted control. Real plants grew amidst the concrete and plastic, giving the area an almost alien smell. Various vehicles were abandoned. Most had smashed windows with bloodstains on the glass, but a minority had their doors left open. Factories and warehouses were in similar disarray; piles of discarded personal effects littered their forecourts. The silence was absolute, save for the occasional call of a bird overhead.

When they reached a small, windowless building John stopped. He looked through a ragged hole in its brickwork and grinned like an infant. Using his binoculars, he'd surveyed the contents of the lock-up prior to departing Asquith. The long-coveted item was still present. 'Here we are,' he enthused.

'Yes, we are,' Frank spoke evenly. 'Are you sure this is a good idea, John? Surely there are quieter, more stealthy options.'

'You're probably right. But remember, Frank, you're motivated by logic. I'm a stupid human. Come on, let's get this door open.'

Frank stood well clear as John used an EMP rod to short the electronic lock. When the doors swung open, motes of dust danced in the wan sunlight. In the gloom was a sight that set John's pulse racing. Frank was less impressed. Even so, the latter set to work without complaint. After casting the guns, they'd instructed the 3D printer to craft a set of automobile tools. Not ones suitable for a modern, electric car, but the type used for internal combustion engines. Hooked up to the Internet for one last time, Frank had downloaded a car mechanic's manual.

Soon enough, the blue auto was ready to drive, its purr loud in the confined space. John and Frank were both grimy with oil and sweat, but neither cared.

The former was like a child, giddy and verbose. 'This, my friend, is a Dodge Viper GTS.' He patted the roof. 'Eight litre V10 engine. Four hundred brake horsepower. One hundred KPH in four and a half seconds. Top speed two hundred and sixty-five kilometres -per-hour. Thing of beauty, ain't she?'

'Hmm.' Frank was unconvinced. 'What's the significance of the twin white stripes on the top?'

'They don't mean anything, purely cosmetic.'

'And how much fuel does it expend? The tank is full, but there's none spare.'

'She's a thirsty girl, I'll admit, but we don't have far to go.'

'It seems very noisy, even when idling. Is this really wise, announcing our approach so emphatically?'

'We've been over this.' John was resolute.

The volume of their arrival wasn't necessarily a negative. As well as alerting zomb-augs, it would also draw the attention of any survivors. John had made his decision, anyway. He'd spent the last year cowering in silence, denying his human urges just to eke out an empty life. He climbed into the driver seat, savouring the moment. He'd long had an enthusiasm for twentieth century automobiles. Lacking the computer technology of their descendants, they were powerful yet obedient. Modern cars were sanitised but sinister. Reflections of a society intent on luxurious self-destruction. 'Open the garage door, please,' he asked Frank, suddenly desperate to leave.

Engine roaring, headlamps glaring, the muscular car responded to John's simulation-honed skills. Once he'd exited the industrial complex, he let the Viper have its head. Save for abandoned vehicles, the city-bound highway was empty. Soon they broke 200kph; John's arms pulsed with energy. The city skyline was forbidding on the horizon, but he increased his speed. Grinning, he turned to Frank. 'What do you think?'

'Of the car?' Frank clarified. 'It has a certain charm, I suppose.'

John laughed. 'It does.'

Chapter 9

They arrived in NYC at dusk. Frank had assessed the footage provided by the haywire UAV, and that posted by POST-AUGPOCALYPSE2067, and he'd studied street view maps. He believed the location of the barrel attacks to be Manhattan, though he wasn't sure. With that in mind, John took the New Jersey Turnpike and crossed the Hudson via the George Washington Bridge. Tonight they would bed down in one of the thousands of empty buildings in the vast metropolis. Their search was to begin at first light tomorrow.

New York City was eerily quiet. The city that didn't sleep wasn't just asleep; it was comatose. The true scale of degradation would be evident in the morning, John knew. Even in the dark, though, the transformation was evident. Amidst the packed buildings and gloom, there was a sense of failure. The biggest and best that humans had ever conceived was now a fallout zone.

John picked an office in mid-Manhattan for their night's stay. Besides a few smashed windows and the absence of electrical power, the premises were in a good state of repair. There were blood splashes on a couple of walls, but no corpses. Once he and Frank had set up camp, using the kitchen in what appeared to have been a legal firm's HQ, John breathed a sigh of relief.

They spent the evening talking about John's last stint in the city. 'They were everywhere,' he said. 'You couldn't travel more than a block without coming across the zombies. I wonder where they've all gone?'

'They've probably gone further afield,' Frank offered.

'What drives them, though? In all the old movies, zombies used to be desperate to eat. That's not the case with ours. But if they're moving, like you say, they must be doing it for a reason.'

'Perhaps they're being controlled by some exterior force.'

'That would make sense. When I was defending Asquith, sometimes they'd seem coordinated, and they'd come in numbers. But at other times, they seemed aimless, as if they'd just wandered my way by chance, and there would only be a couple of them.'

'Did they behave any differently once they'd made it into your compound?'

'I suppose so.' John yawned. He climbed into a sleeping bag. 'When they were coordinated, they were in more of a rush.'

'There will be an explanation.'

'Maybe. Another thing I've been wondering about is the lack of dead bodies. There were still people working here without augs. Cleaners, that sort of thing. A lot of companies preferred to pay them a pittance rather than fork out big lump sums to replace them with AI. So where are their bodies? It was like a slaughterhouse last time I was in NYC, but someone's cleaned up.'

'We will probably answer these questions as we encounter more zomb-augs.' Although Frank didn't need to sleep, he seemed keen to rest.

***

It was a strange sensation that woke John in the dead of night. A moving, twisting, fluid, powerful weight. Every sinew in his body craved flight, but an instinct in his sleep-addled mind cautioned against movement. He opened his eyes. All was dark. Even though the premise defied logic, he knew there was a snake on him. A big snake, a constrictor. A python, perhaps. Adrenaline slowed time. He felt dry scales on his hand, the twitch of individual muscles in the reptile's body. 'Frank,' he whispered.

The snake paused and hissed.

John swallowed. His bowels pulsed.

'Frank!' This time his voice was a touch louder.

Steps sounded from the corridor, and a door opened. The kitchen was slightly less dark, or perhaps John's eyes were adjusting.

The snake started to slither again. By now the bulk of its mass was on John's chest.

'Did you say something, John?' Frank said.

'Yes. There's a snake on me.'

Frank was quiet for a few heartbeats. 'So there is. How curious.' Frank began to approach.

Their guest froze; John sensed tension in its form.

'The fuck are you doing?' John breathed. 'Stop moving, it'll bite me!'

'How should I proceed?

'Just wait till it's off me, then —'

John hushed as he felt a tiny flutter at his throat. A forked tongue flickering against his Adam's apple. The animal's head, short and snub, tickling the flesh under his ear. Probing, slipping between John's shoulder and his inflatable pillow.

It was going to strangle him.

He bit his tongue to prevent himself from crying out. 'Oh god,' he muttered.

The snake was turning, preparing to double back and encircle John's neck.

Didn't snakes strike first, before they constricted? Was it merely passing by? Or was it preying on him?

'Frank, just get it off me. Now. Get this fucking thing off me!'

Frank stepped forwards. He reached down and seized the snake. John pushed himself into a standing position and flattened his back against a wall.

Gripping the snake by two hands – one at either end – Frank stood still for a moment, seemingly at a loss. 'What now, John?'

The snake wriggled, but it was held fast.

'I don't know, just get rid of it!' John watched the beast flex. He opened a window. 'Throw it out!'

Frank, whose facial expression had remained implacable throughout, did as he was told.

John watched the snake disappear into the gloom. From nine storeys, the fall would surely be fatal. 'What the fuck?' he said, closing the window. 'A snake?'

'Yes. A large one, too.' Frank seemed amused. 'I wonder where it came from?'

'Somebody's pet, maybe. There are residential apartments in this building. Solar power's kept the heating on high enough, especially if it nested near the hot water pipes. Must've survived on rats, I suppose.'

***

After that, John couldn't sleep. It was too dark to venture outside, so he and Frank talked. The latter's Internet education hadn't been limited to practical subjects: he'd learnt about politics, philosophy, even religion. Starved of meaningful conversation, John found their dialogue stimulating. He found, however, that the bot did not have many of his own opinions. Frank was able to analyse the views of others and argue for or against, but he didn't lean in either direction. When John commented on said limitation, Frank explained that he would, in time, reach his own conclusions.

***

The morning was bright, the clouds sparse. Armed with plenty of firepower, and with a drone scouting ahead, the explorers set forth. The city streets looked much the same as they did a couple of years ago, though there were plants in peculiar places. Broken glass sparkled in the sunshine; mangled cars were parked haphazardly; shop fronts were seared by long-extinguished fires. But it was the complete absence of pedestrians and traffic which disquieted John the most. The amount of collateral damage was underwhelming in comparison. His and Frank's footsteps were eerily loud against the silence.

Mankind had been defeated without a whimper. There had been no last stand, no final battle. This wasn't Stalingrad in 1943, or Pyongyang, 2053. It was as if the people of New York had simply ceased to exist. A sadness hung above the city like a cloud, along with a smell of decay.

They'd been walking for half a kilometre when the drone alerted Frank. 'Humanoid, next street on the right,' he translated.

Unlike his synthetic friend, John was fearful. He preferred observing zomb-augs from a safe distance.

Frank didn't pause for a second, and John had to hurry to keep up. As the main road gave way to a side street, he flattened himself against the wall of the building on the corner.

But Frank rounded the junction without hesitation.

'Hang on!' John called, following.

The road into which they turned was bathed in sunlight, for there was a gap between skyscrapers up ahead. A bus had crashed into a bus stop; its door yawned. There was no sign of the zomb, but the UAV hovered above the bus. Shotgun ready, Frank skirted the vehicle. John copied, but a few paces back.

Suddenly the zomb-aug lurched into view. It was just ten metres away. John's guts reacted, and he drew his own pistol.

The monster hesitated, cocked its head as it evaluated the threat.

Frank blasted the zomb-aug in the face, spraying brain and bone against the bus's rear window. 'See,' he said, pumping another shell into his weapon. 'No problem.'

'They're not usually that slow,' John insisted, wiping sweaty palms on his trousers. 'Honest.'

'Let's continue.' Frank led the way.

Two blocks later, they encountered another zombie. This one, loitering outside a department store, was quicker to respond, but its fate was the same. The third fell to John's handgun, an easy kill; the creature had been absorbed by the corpse of a dog. It wasn't eating. It was merely poking at the animal's innards.

'Something's not right,' John said. Unaccustomed to exercise, he stopped to lean against a parked car. 'These aren't like the ones who've attacked the compound. They're... useless. Aimless.'

'There will be an explanation.' Frank took a moment to reload his shotgun, and then he stood still, his eyes blank. 'Still no reported signs of human life from the drone. Perhaps we've got the wrong area.'

'No, I'm sure it was around here. You said so yourself.'

'They could've moved. Wouldn't we be better using the car to patrol the streets? We'd cover more ground.'

'Perhaps.' John sighed. Why had he thought this mission would be straightforward? They were searching one of the biggest cities on Earth for a handful of people.

By noon, John needed a break and something to eat. Systematically, they'd scoured several miles of Manhattan's avenues, alleyways and squares without finding anyone. They'd killed forty or so zomb-augs, economically. All but two of which were alone, though the pair posed no more of a threat than their lonesome peers. Lamenting the decision to leave the car at the office, which had been taken with fuel economy in mind, they'd tried to commandeer a couple of cars. Neither had started. Their electrics were fried, probably by EMPs, Frank said.

While John ate, sat on a bench, Frank focussed on piloting the drone. He spied through windows, entered unsecured buildings and retraced their steps to ensure they'd not missed anything. He also noted that every subway station entrance was locked.

Before leaving Asquith, John had prepared dozens of recyclo-meals, while Frank had concentrated on the firearms and ammunition. John's lunch tasted like flavoured cardboard. However, it was sufficiently appetising to entice a pigeon from the rafters of a nearby building. Without thinking, John threw a scrap of food for the bird. It was beaten to the morsel by, of all things, a monkey, which had descended from a bus shelter.

'Look, Frank!'

'Hmm.' The cyborg regarded the animal as it climbed a tree and munched its snack. 'New York has never been renowned for its primate population, has it?'

'No,' John chuckled. 'Perhaps it's a pet, like the snake.' He broke off another piece of his wrap and tried to lure the critter down to the ground.

The monkey was wary, though. It chattered at its audience, then leapt to another tree.

Before long, its caution was explained. From the east approached a zomb-aug, a coffee-skinned male in a police uniform. Two more came from the opposite direction.

Ignoring the shivers that ran down his spine, John stood, pistol ready. 'Perhaps stopping was a bad idea,' he said.

'Perhaps.' Frank raised his shotgun and faced the pair from the west. 'It's not a problem. We can fight them all day in these quantities.'

Taking aim, John prepared to kill the single zombie, which growled as it quickened its pace. John waited until it was ten metres away. He was about to shoot when the monkey vocalised once more, distracting him. Behind him Frank fired. There was a gasp as the shot hit its mark. By now John's target was almost on top of him. He automatically backed away and let off a round, catching the monster on the right shoulder.

The zomb was knocked out of its stride, but it kept coming. Arms reached for John's face. Teeth bared. The stench was fetid.

Frank fired again.

As did John. Except he did so in a panic, and his bullet wasted itself in the zombie's left arm.

Unfazed, the thing grabbed John's right arm. Its grip was iron; the pistol dropped to the floor.

'Move, John!' Frank yelled, the words distorted as if uttered through water. The clunk-click of his weapon's pump-action was surreally slow.

The zomb-aug seized John's left wrist and simultaneously lunged at the human with its teeth.

John closed his eyes and roared, half from fear, half from anger.

And then, suddenly, the zombie attacking John was plucked from its feet. Such was the strength of his foe that John was pulled to the ground as his would-be murderer was toppled. John struggled to free himself, prising away the dirty fingers holding his arms. He crawled away and reached for his handgun.

A noise made gave him pause.

Flesh tearing in strong jaws. The crunch of bone.

John turned.

Chapter 10

On top of the zomb was a lithe, black, beautiful bundle of muscle.

A panther. A fucking panther!

It looked at John for a moment, a warning in its eyes. Blood dripped from its fangs as it peered into the man's soul. Then it snarled, a surprisingly high-pitched sound for such a powerful predator. After what felt like an eon, the big cat broke eye contact and started to drag its prey away.

No longer mesmerised, John jumped to his feet and ran, barely registering Frank as he passed him by. He flew past the two zomb-augs Frank had slain, though he almost slipped in the mess of one's ruptured cranium. And he continued sprinting until his lungs and legs forced him to stop. He stood panting for a minute, watching the direction from which he'd come. Feeling faint, he leaned on the railings of a small park, at the corner of West 9th Street and 6th Avenue. His senses were heightened: birds chirped; winds from north and east competed; and there was a faint miasma of sewage.

Soon enough, Frank arrived. He'd retrieved John's gun, and he handed it back. 'Is everything alright, John?' he asked, head tilted condescendingly.

'No,' John wheezed. 'Since I woke up, I've been attacked by a snake, a zombie and now, a fucking black panther. So no, everything is *not* alright.'

'Technically, John, neither the snake nor the black panther attacked you as such. They just scared you.'

John blinked. His hand suddenly ached; he'd been gripping the iron fence too hard.

'Did you know, John, that the term "panther" is something of a misnomer? Panthers are simply black jaguars or leopards. Judging by the method of attack that one employed, and its size, I'd say it was a jaguar. Jaguars kill their prey by biting the skull, you know.'

'I think I left you hooked up to the Internet too long.'

***

It was time to get off the streets. They needed to regroup and consider their next move. Groups of zomb-augs and escapees from the city zoo weren't conducive to strategic planning. For once fortune favoured them; they happened upon a luxury hotel in the East Village. Thanks to a solar-powered generator, many of its facilities were still in working order. Most pleasing was its stock of long-life food. The larder attached to the kitchen was replete with tinned goodness, and John ate the tastiest lunch he'd had in months. There were even napkins to wipe his face clean of soup and sauce.

Leaving Frank to continue his drone-aided search of the borough, John explored the building. Some of the rooms were in a state of disarray, with curtains torn to the floor, holo-jectors smashed and mirrors cracked. There were dark stains on corridor carpets and corresponding blood patterns on the walls. Personal belongings – wallets, ID cards, handbags – were left in most of the suites. There was a smell of death in the air; it wasn't something John noticed straightaway, rather an impression he gained the longer he spent in the hotel.

John was about to head back to the lobby and meet Frank when he found a room that had, at some point, been barricaded. The door hung from one hinge. He had to climb over a pile of furniture that had obviously been used to prevent the door being breached. On the linoleum floor was the largest bloodstain he'd seen thus far. It was a small chamber, maybe three metres square, and it appeared to have been an office at some point. A dirty mattress was pushed against the right hand wall, a desk and chair on the opposite side. Empty drink and food cans completed the scene. John was most interested in the holo-jector and wrist-com on the bureau, both of which looked to be undamaged.

It didn't take long to synch the wrist-com with the holo-jector. For an agonising moment John feared the com's memory had been corrupted, for there was no visual, just sound. Then he realised the file was audio only. It was a man's journal. John hit play.

'My name is Marco Wochowski. I'm a bellboy at Arcadia Heights, one of the last humans doing jobs like this. People laughed at me, you know, when I said "no" to augs. They said, "Marco, you crazy? You inherited all that credit, you can afford the best techno-shit in the world. And you're gonna work a menial job, be treated like a chump?" Now who's laughing? Now who's paranoid? Last night, it happened. The world went to shit. Real, apocalyptic, end-of-the-world shit went down. Everyone died at the same time, and then everyone came back to life at the same time. But not really back to life. Because they're all fucking zombies! Except me. Now who's laughing?"

Aptly, Marco finished his monologue with a peal of laughter that bordered on maniacal. Silence, and then:

'Day four. Ventured outside for the first time since weekend. Big mistake. There's dead bodies everywhere. Humans, dogs, cats, you name it. Virtually all the dead people have one thing in common. They're poor. Well, they work poor people jobs. But I suppose I do, too, and I'm not poor. So they're either poor, or clued in, like yours truly. Don't think they're as smart as me, though, because they're all dead and I'm alive. Those zombies, though, they ain't smart. Scary, but dumb as fuck.
'Day seven. When I said last time "they're all dead" I was wrong. But now I'm not. Because I haven't seen another living soul for days. Dude came here the other day, said he was part of some "collective," and they were getting out of the city. I said I'd think about it, even though I knew I wouldn't. So they came here last night in a big truck, whole buncha them, and they were waiting for me outside. But then, must've been about a hundred zombies showed up. The dude and his crew couldn't get away in time, and they were screwed, all of them. Feel kinda bad now.
'Day nine. Real hungry now, but scared to leave the room. What do they want? The zombies, I mean. They don't eat people, so they ain't hunting for food. They're not looking for territory, because they always fuck off when they've killed everyone. No one's in charge, as far as I can see. All they want to do is kill and smash shit up. How do you beat that? They'll find me soon, they've got to. Then I'm fucked. Real fucked.'

There were no more entries. John sat for a moment, a familiar hollow feeling in his bosom. Like Marco, he'd been marooned in the city, surrounded by panicking humans and relentless zombies. He recalled the despair as each of his friends was butchered. The false dawns when it seemed they'd outrun their nemesis, only to have another hideout exposed and conquered. And, most of all, the confusion. Why were the zomb-augs so intent on destroying humans? Who was directing the culling? Who'd caused the zomb-augpocalypse? Why? Of course, these questions still troubled John, but he'd come to terms with the likelihood that he would never be enlightened.

Not that he didn't have theories. He'd considered various culpable parties, and he was of the mind that the AI Council were responsible for the current state of affairs. They'd been created to oppose the roboticisation of the world, offering people a means to remain relevant by augmenting themselves. Whether they'd deliberately released the computer virus or it'd been an accident was another question. Although there wasn't an obvious motive for the Council to target augmentees, it seemed too much of a coincidence that they'd pushed so hard for augmentation, only for it to lead to the end of civilisation.

Hearing Marco's tale left John emotionally exhausted. He wiped tears from his eyes and stood. Suddenly he felt tired, the kilometres travelled taking their toll. He'd been running on hope; now he realised that most non-augs would've met the same fate as Marco.

When they met in the lobby, Frank immediately detected his master's change of demeanour. 'Is everything okay, John?'

'Yeah, fine,' he brusquely replied. 'Any luck with the drone hunt?'

'No, I'm afraid not. Of course, I've only done an initial sweep so far.'

'I'm wondering if we should've prepared better before we set out. Researched the city, looked at the most viable areas for humans to live. Because we're sort of flying blind, here, just scrabbling about, hoping to hit the jackpot.'

'Hmm.' Frank scratched his head. A gesture he must've learned. 'So we need somewhere else with Internet access.'

'Yeah.' John kicked his heels against the front desk against which he leant.

'Like Asquith Robotic?'

'Yeah. I mean, we wouldn't go back there for good, just till we know what we need to know.'

'Sure. Well, it's your call. But I still think I can find them using the drone. I've surveilled most of Manhattan now.'

'But what if they've moved somewhere else in New York? It's a big city, Frank. Crazy idea, now I think about it, just wandering around like this.'

***

Back outside, John felt more paranoid. Perhaps having a goal – finding the gang of survivors – had distracted him from fear. Or the dead man's account had spooked him. Paradoxically, his trepidation was worsened by quieter streets. Before their brief stop at the hotel, they'd encountered zombaugs with increasing frequency. Now they were totally alone. Their route to the office where they'd spent the previous night took them longer than anticipated. Many of the Midtown Manhattan roads were barricaded at the most inopportune points.

Eventually they reached Times Square. Two year-old litter swirled in an increasingly-strong breeze. Weeds that'd grown through cracks in paving stones swayed. Birds landed on crashed taxi bonnets, eyed the human and his companion, and then took to the air once more. To John the atmosphere seemed leaden. Perhaps the newly-arrived steel-grey clouds were to blame, but a primal part of him attributed the tension to the paranormal.

In this place, just twenty-three months ago, between the now-blank billboards and high-rises, hundreds perished simultaneously. The pacemakers controlled by their aug suites, falsely sold as a solution to heart disease, malfunctioned. Then, minutes later, the fallen got up and wreaked havoc. As he walked 7th Avenue, John tried to imagine the scene. A shiver shot down his spine. 'It must've been horrific here,' he said, his voice barely above a whisper.

'Do you mean when the virus hit?' Frank asked. Insensitive to drops in air pressure and the heebie-jeebies, the cyborg was untroubled by the environs.

'Yeah. Just imagine being a non-aug, seeing so many people drop to the ground. Going to help them, only for them to jump up and start killing.'

'I imagine it was very distressing.'

John fell silent for a moment. Then he laughed. 'Yeah, "very distressing" is one way of putting it.'

'You didn't see any of that? When the virus hit?'

'No. I slept through it, believe it or not.' He chuckled again, this time too heartily.

By this time they'd reached West 58th, just one intersection from Central Park. The trees enticed John; he longed to escape the concrete maze and its ghosts. The prospect of running into the park zoo's grizzly bear played on his mind, but Frank had assured him he would be ready.

A fat drop of rain landed on John's arm, then another on his head. The wind was building, while thunder rumbled in the distance. 'We need to find shelter,' he said, almost to himself.

But as they approached the junction of 7th and West 59th, inclement weather became the last of John's worries. Suddenly, the route to the park was being blocked. Zombaugs came from both directions on West 59th. At least twenty from the northwest, the same number from the southeast. John gaped as the monsters formed two lines, like a company of Napoleonic-era soldiers. They wobbled a little as they waited, their arms outstretched. Blackened teeth were bared; eyes stared. But, somehow, the monsters maintained discipline.

Stomach sinking, John turned. The manoeuvre had been replicated by zombs on West 58th Street. A hundred metres separated the two formations, with John and Frank just twenty metres from the northernmost.

They were trapped.

A fork of lightning split the sky to the south, and, seconds later, the thunder answered. The heavens opened.

Chapter 11

Although John's first urge was to vomit, he instructed himself to remain calm. Frank wasted no time, drawing his pistol and headshotting a couple of the freaks that blocked their route to the park. They fell, entry wounds spurting blood, but their places in the front rank were taken by the ones behind. Two more zombies approached from 59th to reinforce the cordon.

And still, the ungodly host did not advance. They, or whoever was controlling them, seemed content to hold their quarry in place.

Taking more care in order to compensate for the longer range, Frank blasted a pair of the zombs to the southwest. They were replaced in the same manner as the first couple.

'What now?' John's voice wavered. He wiped his eyes clear of rain and sweat.

'I've recalled the recon UAV, should be here in thirty seconds. I doubt it'll be enough on its own, but I've activated and summoned UAVs two and three, they'll be with us shortly.' Frank aimed again at the closest foes but opted not to fire. 'They can help us shoot our way through to the park.'

'Why didn't the drone spot these hostiles?'

'I don't know, John. I've been checking the feeds and I've seen nothing. It's as if they've come from nowhere.'

Just then, a comforting buzz sounded from above. The drone had arrived. It descended to an altitude of five metres, its guns pointing in the direction of Central Park.

And then, as if in response, came zombie reinforcements from 59th West. Within thirty seconds, the enemy's number had doubled. The majority blocked the way back to the office and the car. Newcomers continued to arrive at a trickle. But, even with their overwhelming advantage, the zombs kept their distance.

'What are they doing?' John wondered. Bemusement was trumping terror now.

'I don't know.' Frank looked at the skies expectantly. 'They're giving us more time, though. Drones two and three are less than a minute away.'

A sound to their rear grabbed John's attention. The odds were getting worse: approximately thirty more zombies had joined 7th from West 58th. The sea of undead was now advancing, slowly closing the distance between themselves and the two intruders on their patch. As they moved they grumbled and fretted, as if vexed by their invisible restraints. Meanwhile, their friends at the end of the road, the anvil to their hammer, whose ranks were swelling by the moment, were motionless.

John's heart pounded in his ears. Incontinence was imminent, though the rainfall was so heavy that he doubted he'd feel his own piss. He was ready to sink to his knees when the whirr of drones two and three gave him hope. 'Now, Frank, let's blast our way through. We only have to create a corridor —'

Machine guns drowned out his voice. Concentrating their fire on the right-hand side of the thoroughfare, the three drones, controlled by Frank, decimated the horde. For a moment John was fixated, unable to ignore the slaughter. Thousands of rounds carved a gory channel through the morass of exposed humanoids. And then the drones stopped firing.

'Run, John!' Frank repeated.

And he did. Skidding on blood and entrails, he dashed through the gap.

Twice he heard Frank's shotgun behind him when unharmed zomb-augs managed to clamber over the corpses of their fallen comrades and pose a threat. A hand clutched John's ankle just as he made it onto West 59th; he turned and shotgunned the crawling beast without hesitation.

At the junction, he realised their bacon was yet to be saved. He and Frank were no longer contained, but their UAVs were out of ammo. They weren't designed for prolonged fire-fights. And, judging by the stream of zombs from Central Park, it was not the sanctuary he'd hoped for. At least they had room to dodge, though, and that's what he and Frank did. As they took West Drive into the park, they danced past countless attackers, shooting those that got too close.

Frank was tireless. He was beginning to put distance between himself and John, who hopped a fence and ran across a children's playground. The human's feet were wet from puddles; rain was in his eyes. But at least the zombies were sparser. 'Wait!' he called.

'Sorry,' Frank shouted, pausing at the edge of the Sheep Meadow. While he waited, he shot a zomb-aug nearby. Then he sniped one that was heading to intercept his master.

When John caught up, they had a moment to take stock. 'Where next, Frank?'

'Carry on to the other side, I think, and hope there's some breathing space on that side.' Frank reloaded both of his guns, prompting John to do likewise. 'Are you ready to continue?'

Side by side they trudged across the field. The grass was long, their steps muffled. On three occasions zombs sighted them from Center Drive. Each time Frank stopped them with long range pistol shots. On the north side of the meadow, the trees were thicker. The sun was now beaming through a gap in the clouds, but its rays were stymied by the leaves and branches above. Skirting the boating lake, the refugees headed north. Their pace was deliberate, stealthy, for the zombies were less numerous and could be evaded altogether with enough care.

At one point the undergrowth was too dense, meaning they had to rejoin the path. Two zombs were up ahead. They swayed slightly, like nightclub revellers without the confidence to join the dance floor.

'My map indicates that we can get to within ten metres of them, then switch to the lane running parallel to avoid them.' Frank's eyes went blank for a moment. 'It's best we don't fire any unnecessary shots, they seem sensitive to noise.'

They were within fifteen metres when the ground collapsed beneath their feet. John landed painfully on his backside and ended up on his back, face to face with the charred face of a zomb-aug. He let out an involuntary yell of fright, whereas Frank took the fall more stoically.

'What the fuck?' the former hissed. His heart felt ready to burst. About two and a half metres deep, and four metres in width, the trench was sheer-sided. At their feet were the carcasses of three zombs, their flesh scorched black. The twigs and branches that'd hidden the hole were scattered across the ground.

Frank appraised the earthern walls of the pit. 'It appears we are trapped.'

'No shit. Do you think they heard me shout?'

'Probably.'

'Can you not jump out? I mean, you run fast, your aim is awesome. You're practically a superhero.'

'That's right. So I can do things humans do far better. But humans don't tend to jump vertically, so nor do I.'

'There must be a way out.' John began scouring the sides of the excavation, scrabbling at the soil, hoping to find a tree root to aid his ascent. 'Come on, Frank, help.'

'I'm thinking,' the bot chided. Then his voice dropped. 'John. Stop moving. Be quiet.'

The man's irritation quickly turned to anxiety when he followed Frank's gaze. Just a few feet above them, at ground level, stood a zombie. It was still for a moment. It shifted a few centimetres, blocking out the sun. Dirt particles, disturbed by the monster's boots, fell into John's gaping mouth. He stifled a cough. Sixty seconds passed; the zomb remained on the edge of the trap. Not quite teetering, but close enough to hear the working of its jaws.

And then it looked down. It registered the hapless pair below. Before Frank could bring his shotgun to bear and blow it away, it let out a loud growl.

John winced at the weapon's din. 'Shit.'

Frank shrugged. 'What else could I do?'

A minute later, the trench was surrounded. At least twenty undead fiends stared down at their elusive prize.

Nostrils flared, jaw set, John pumped another shell into his shotgun.

Chapter 12

The first zomb-aug dived into the pit.

John fired and missed, but his shot hit one of the others at the edge.

Diving zomb landed on Frank, flattening him.

For a split second, John was torn between saving his robot and stopping the next monster. Then he realised that the one on top of Frank wasn't attacking – it was dead weight. A short black bolt protruded from the base of its skull.

Another zomb fell into the trench. Speared by the same sort of projectile, it was as dead as its predecessor.

'What the fuck?' John helped the cyborg to his feet.

A third zombie fell into the hole. It was still "alive," having been shot in the small of the back.

Frank and John finished it off with a barrage of shotgun fire and looked upwards. The zomb-augs had disappeared, presumably to face their attackers.

The music of smashing glass was instantly followed by the sound of igniting fuel, and at least two distinct inhuman screeches. Plus the stench of roasting flesh. Again a figure obscured the sun, but this one added rather than reduced illumination. Bathed in flames, the beast flapped at itself for a couple of heartbeats then plunged into the trapping pit, narrowly missing John. 'Watch out!' he pleaded, not knowing if he would be heard.

Perhaps his protest was heeded, because only one more burning beast toppled into the hollow. A minute or two passed. Suddenly the light was blocked again. Around the lip of the concealed pit trap were ten humans, each carrying a weapon. The woman who'd posted the fire-barrel video was there.

Crossbow in hand, she said, 'I suppose we'd better get you out.'

***

'So are we prisoners, or not?' John asked. His wrists weren't bound; the crew had lowered their crossbows, bows and catapults. However, he and Frank had been told to walk ahead of their escort. Thanks to the brisk pace set by the armed gang, his heart rate was yet to recover from the near-fatal chase from Times Square to Central Park.

'You're not,' video-woman said. 'Not yet, anyway.'

'What does that mean? "Not yet."'

'It means it's not our choice.' A gruff-voiced man, roughly thirty years of age, had spoken. He walked closest to a slightly younger male of similar appearance. 'The chief will decide.'

'Who's the chief?'

'You'll find out soon enough,' said a girl in her late teens.

Frank kept his own counsel.

John was about to ask another question, but he opted to remain silent. Instead he stole occasional glances at the men and women to his rear. When he and Frank were first extricated from the wolf hole, using ropes, he'd paid particular attention to the group's necks. Including video-woman, three of the ten had the scar that indicated removal of aug chips.

The other two with scars – the teenaged girl and a young man of about the same age – acted no differently to their friends.

All ten were dressed in bizarre fashion. Their apparel was leather-dominated, on the verge of fetishism. They were seemingly fond of belts, bandoliers and straps, anything from which equipment could be hung. Most clothing and accessories were in shades of grey, the colour of concrete. Seven males, three females, all under the age of forty. The men had beards. The women had functionally-short hair. Six of the collective were white or Hispanic; two were black; two Asian. They laughed and joked as they walked through the park, complimenting or deriding each other on their performance during the skirmish.

One of them, probably the eldest and definitely the largest, produced a small cardboard box, from which he drew an old-fashioned tobacco cigarette. Without breaking stride, he used a match to ignited the cig and puffed a plume of smoke. When he saw John watching, fascinated, he offered him the pack.

John shook his head but carried on watching as he walked. He'd seen the archaic practice only in movies, and his incredulity must've shown on his face. All cancers were curable; at least, they would be if there were any doctors alive. Even so, electronic methods of consuming stimulants were now ubiquitous.

'I know, I know,' the big fellow said with a crooked smile. His teeth were dazzlingly-white against his mahogany skin. 'They'll kill me sure as any zombie, and it'll probably hurt more. But we don't trust electricity. Not too much. Hence the bikes.'

'Bikes?'

The man pointed straight ahead: the exit onto Adam Clayton Powell Jr was a hundred metres away. John could just about see a collection of bicycles at the foot of a mighty tree.

'Do you have any spares?' John asked, already knowing his question was foolish.

One of the women, a spiky-haired Oriental with five short knives fastened to her belt, chortled and said, 'I hope those shoes are comfortable.'

John's head dropped. Bikes meant a journey too long to make on foot.

'Don't worry,' video-woman said. 'You can climb on the back of mine.'

'No, I can walk, I'll be fine —'

'No you won't. Don't argue, we haven't got time. The streets are still crawling with freaks.' Her tone brooked no debate. She set off at a jog in the direction of their cycles, followed by three of the gang, including the younger of the pair who appeared to be related. Using hand signals, she directed three others to veer to the right. They responded at a sprint, leaving three of the warriors – the giant African-American, the Chinese woman and the elder of the maybe-relatives – to accompany the newcomers at a more leisurely speed.

'Has she said anything about the machine?' the last of the trio asked. He strolled with an arrogance which belied his diminutive stature.

'What about it?' spiky-hair said.

'It'll slow us down.' He eyed Frank with contempt, as had most of his gang-mates thus far.

'The machine will be just fine,' Frank said, raising a hand to stop John interjecting. 'I can run at over thirty kilometres per hour for three hours before I need to slow to a jog.'

'Impressive,' the biggest man said. 'What's your energy source?'

'A combination of solar power and self-generated kinetic energy.'

'Like perpetual motion?' the Oriental woman asked. She walked sideways for a few paces and stared at Frank. 'That's some sinister shit right there.'

'That's why we fear the machines,' big guy said. He plucked his bike from the floor like it was a toy. 'Faster, stronger, better. Unless they've got a steel bolt in their brain.' He clinked his crossbow against one of the Chinese woman's daggers. 'Ain't that right?'

'Damn right.' She cut the air with her blade.

'Enough chatter,' video-woman ordered, sat on her bicycle. 'We're waiting for you.'

The trio who'd forged ahead with her were already mounted. Those that'd scouted to the right were just arriving.

'Go where?' John asked, his mind a whirl.

'You'll find out soon enough.' She shifted her position in order for him to mount her bike.

'Wouldn't it be better if the big bloke gave me a ride?'

'Why, because I'm a weak female? Just get on.' She looked past John and frowned.

John followed her gaze.

The two guys who looked alike had not yet mounted up, but were instead conversing quietly. The elder glared at John for a moment.

'Is there a problem?' Video-woman squinted in the afternoon sun.

'Yeah,' the younger said, arms folded. 'We can't take the machine with us.'

Bridling, John took a step towards them. 'He's with me. He doesn't go, I don't go.'

'Fine with us,' the elder said, hands on hips.

'Chief wouldn't be happy,' one of the others agreed. Close to two metres in height but lanky in build, he spoke with a New Orleans accent. His dark skin was stretched too tightly on his bones.

The teenaged girl nodded; her curls bounced. 'You know how he feels about them.'

'Well I'm in charge when he's not here. You know that. And I say they're both coming. You can take it up with Chief if you want. Now let's go before a patrol shows up.'

Briefly the pair glowered, the younger stretching the elastic of his slingshot, the elder licking his lips. Then, as if by telepathy, they simultaneously stood down.

'Thanks.' John climbed onto the leader's bike. He gripped the seat beneath him with both hands.

'No problem.' She began to pedal; the rest followed suit.

Looking over her shoulder, John saw her thigh muscles bulge with the initial effort required to get them moving.

***

They'd travelled northwards for about half an hour when John mustered the courage to speak. 'Where did they come from, the zombs? The streets were empty, then *bam!* They were everywhere.'

'The subway.' The woman was barely out of breath.

'You think they... recharge down there?'

'What do you mean?'

'They're geothermically-powered, aren't they?'

'I guess.'

'So, really, where are we going?'

'Our home.'

John grinned. 'Which is *where*, exactly?'

'About another fifteen k from here.'

'And where is here?'

She huffed. 'We're on Route 87, just short of Kingsbridge, the Bronx. To the right is Jerome Park Reservoir.'

A strip of green lay to the east, next to an expanse of water. Birds wheeled above the trees; wind tickled the overgrown grass.

'It seems pretty quiet out here. No zombs. Why ride all this way into a dangerous city?'

'We spotted your drones with our telescope.' Her voice was feminine yet confident. 'When we see signs of survivors in the city, we try and help.'

'Well, thank you.' John looked to his left: Frank was pounding away on the pavement, arms and legs like pistons. 'You risk your lives to save others.'

'Yeah. I suppose sometimes the apocalypse brings out the best in people.'

For reasons unknown, this statement made John laugh. He worried that his mirth had offended her at first, and then he heard her chuckle. 'Are you honestly not going to tell me your name?' he asked.

'Honestly. Not yet, anyway. You'll thank me if I die. And before you start, don't tell me anything about yourself.'

'Okay. But I can't call you POST-AUGPOCALYPSE2067, can I?'

'No. Do me a favour, don't mention the video in front of the others. We're not supposed to use tech.'

'Sure.'

She went on to explain their philosophy. Three years back, she joined the organisation known as the AugFrees. She was attracted by the idea of a simpler existence, without the trappings and pressures of modern life. Initiation involved sacrifice. All members had their augmentation control chips removed – if they'd had them installed in the first place. Their charismatic chief, Silas Crowe, promised that one day the surgery would save their lives. And so it had. Since the rise of the zomb-augs, the cult's numbers had dwindled. One-by-one, the AugFrees had been killed by zombs or disease.

Half in jest, John wondered aloud if he'd been rescued to boost membership.

'Don't get ahead of yourself,' video-woman cautioned. 'Silas is unpredictable. He might not like you, and he definitely won't like your bot.'

John thought for a moment. 'What about you? Do you "like" me?'

She said nothing, but pedalled a little harder.

'I don't mean "like" me in that way,' he stammered. 'I just mean, would you object to me being with you? All of you, I mean.' John was thankful she couldn't see him blush.

'I know what you mean. Just thought I'd let you squirm a minute. Anyway, you sure you'd *want* to join us?'

Truthfully, John hadn't thought of the future beyond finding POST-AUGPOCALYPSE2067. He wasn't sure he wanted to join Silas's sect, but what was the alternative? Wandering around a desolate United States with only his faithful cyborg for company. Although video-woman and her team were an odd bunch, John was so lonely that he would've joined a cell of Pro-Church terrorists rather than face another day alone. Also, he needed a woman. He'd never been the type to let his baser urges govern his decisions, but this was different. Procreation would be beneficial for the depleted human race. The fact that the object of his affections was attractive and feisty was a bonus.

'Anyway,' the would-be future mother of his children said, 'We're stopping here for a moment.'

"Here" was a rundown neighbourhood, with evidence of rampaging zomb-augs everywhere. Smashed bus shelters, battered shop fronts, overturned cars, dark patches on the asphalt. A fine drizzle had begun to fall; the temperature was lower. The crew stood their bikes against the railings surrounding a basketball court. Meanwhile, Frank stood stock still, his eyes closed.

Elder brother looked at the bot and spat on the ground.

'Down for a game?' the big man asked John, nodding at the stray ball in the centre of the basketball court.

'I... I've never really played,' John began. 'Shouldn't we...'

'Fucking with you, man. Never played myself, either.'

Spiky-hair giggled.

'Why've we stopped, *boss*?' The younger brother had mockery in his eyes. 'Nobody's got a puncture.'

'I know,' video-woman said. 'Just tired of pedalling for two, is all.' She crossed the road. Fishing in her pocket, she retrieved a key and unlocked the only door on the street which hadn't been kicked in or ripped off. Once an augmentation-loan brokers – one of the many that'd been opened over the last half-decade – it now served as a storage depot for the AugFrees.

'Kinda ironic, ain't it?' the beanpole gang member observed. 'Us AugFrees using a place like that as a safe house.'

'No, it's not,' the teenager replied. 'Like I say *every fucking time* you say that. That's not what ironic means, you fucking idiot.'

The semantically-challenged man's protests were interrupted by the return of his temporary commander. 'Here you go,' she said, pushing a pink bike over to John. 'I hope you've been keeping fit.'

***

Of course, John hadn't looked after his physique. So the next hour was perhaps the most punishing of his life. When they arrived at the tower block on the outskirts of Yonkers, NY, he was as sweaty as he was pained. Deep down, though, he felt exhilarated. He was too fatigued to evaluate the locale; it was like any other suburban setting.

Video-woman returned his grin as she ushered him into the building. The others had already entered while he was leaning against a wall, regaining his composure. 'Well,' she said, 'you did good. But you'll need to toughen up. Silas doesn't like passengers.'

'Surely he's not so bad?' John said. 'I mean, he's sort of a good Samaritan, isn't he?'

'Sort of. Sorry, the elevator's fucked. It'll have to be the stairs, but we're only on the sixth floor.'

John almost whimpered.

'Silas is… Silas. You'll meet him soon.'

'You never know, we might get on.'

Video-woman snorted. 'Do you have many friends who've been to cryo-pen for murder?'

Chapter 13

John woke shivering and perspiring. For a few seconds he panicked. Where was he? Then he saw the sliver of light at the bottom of the blackout blind covering the window, and he recalled: he was in an apartment on the sixth floor of a tower block in Yonkers, NY.

A metallic sound in the next room set his pulse racing. It was followed by other clinks and clatters; they were domestic noises. Someone was preparing food. Nothing to fear. So why was he so anxious? Certainly, the twenty-four hours in Manhattan had been stressful, downright terrifying at times, but he'd been through worse. Was his psyche damaged beyond repair? Were the cracks meeting, ready to shatter?

He'd had another nightmare. Another distorted caricature of events as they happened the year before last. Not worse than the truth, just different, a dramatisation. He made to sit up in bed, wincing at the pain in his muscles. Briefly he worried that the dream had hurt him, somehow, until he realised that the cycle upstate was responsible for his aches. He decided to lie still. Maybe someone would bring him refreshment and medication.

No, John resolved, gritting his teeth as he swung his legs off the mattress. He was fine. Three consecutive nights without opiates were taking their toll, as was a general lack of rest. Luckily, he'd only ever used synthetic drugs, not the authentic poppy seed version. Withdrawal wouldn't be as severe as it was for real addicts, like the ones at Rehab Valley. He had a sudden, vivid flashback of the trip he and Antonia had taken to the reality theme park at the turn of the decade. It was a cruel fad, the exploitation of suffering – all in the name of social conscience and philanthropy, supposedly – but most depressing was the fact that no one had truly objected. Perhaps the world deserved the zomb-augpocalypse.

His sleep wasn't helped by the Silas revelation. Afterwards, whilst chatting with video-woman, she'd admitted to exaggerating a little. Although she wouldn't go into detail, she'd promised that "Chief" wasn't a coldblooded killer. His was a complicated story, one he didn't enjoy discussing.

Like most of the conversations John had had so far, it'd ended prematurely. Video-woman was taciturn, as were the others while she was around.

To his surprise, John missed Frank. The bot was to be kept in isolation until Silas returned, a condition of their admittance to the AugFree base. It would only be for a few days, video-woman had said. John sulked nonetheless; Frank seemed indifferent. Accustomed to autonomy, the former was still irked by the decision, though he knew it was a small concession.

Shaking his head, John stood. The stiffness wasn't as bad as he'd expected. He raised the blind by half a metre and reappraised his new quarters. Plainly-furnished yet comfortable, it would suffice for now. Besides, he might soon be sharing someone else's bed. Last night, he'd almost made a pass at video-woman; thankfully, prudence had come to the rescue. He'd never been a lothario, preferring to let friendships develop into romances. But the year on his own had put things into perspective. There was a certain chemistry between them, and he intended to press the issue at some point.

Once he'd learnt her name.

It was barely eight AM, so John tiptoed out of his apartment and knocked on next door.

'Hold up,' a deep voice called. Bolts were shifted, keys turned, and the big African-American answered. He didn't ask John in, but he left the door open.

An odour wafted into the corridor; it reminded John of his greats grandparents' house. He hadn't smelled real meat for an age.

'Guess you'll want some breakfast, huh?'

'That'd be cool, thanks,' John replied, following the tantalising aroma. 'If it's not too much trouble.'

'If it was,' the larger man rumbled, 'you wouldn't get none, but I'm cooking anyway. Make yourself at home. Won't take much longer.'

John took a seat while his host went back to the kitchen. This apartment had the same layout as his, but it was more personalised, with family photographs and souvenirs of foreign holidays adorning the walls and surfaces. There was even a crucifix above the exit door.

'Do you want sauce?' the big man called from the kitchen.

'Sure,' John answered, engrossed by the plethora of personal effects. One photo showed its owner in formal wear, with his huge arm around the shoulders of a woman in a wedding dress. Both bride and bridegroom beamed at the camera. A legend beneath the image read, "Su & Tristan -

April 9th 2058." John picked up the ornately-framed picture and took a closer look: it was 2D, printed on paper, without the facility to zoom in or rotate. Even so, it was more authentic than any of the holo-mems he had.

'Yep.' Tristan was stood in the doorway with a plate in each hand. 'That's me and my lady, the lord rest her soul. Here's your breakfast, bacon sandwich with real bread, real meat, real ketchup.'

'Thanks, Tristan,' John said, mouth watering.

'Just call me T. Everybody else does. Was gonna tell you my name anyway, don't agree with all this secrecy bullshit.'

'I'm John,' he said through a mouthful of food.

'Pleased to meet you, John.'

For a moment they ate in silence; it was the tastiest food John'd ever had.

'You lose anyone?' asked T.

'Yeah, I guess so. Haven't seen my family for years.'

'Shit. Like that, huh? You were the black sheep that escaped the wolves.'

'Hmm.' John finished the first half of his sandwich. 'Doesn't feel like I escaped, sometimes.'

'Oh, you escaped, my friend. Being one of them is a fate worse than death.'

There was a knock at the door. 'Just me,' a female called.

'Coming,' T yelled.

Spiky-haired girl joined them, a bundle of energy. 'Get those blinds open. You got any bacon left?'

'*You* open them. And yeah, your breakfast is ready, going cold quick.'

Spiky-hair talked so much that John wondered how she managed to eat. When she learnt that he and T were on first name terms, she revealed her own. 'Caitlin. But call me Cait.'

The three shared their stories.

T, aged fifty-one, was a veteran of the Marine Corps. He'd fought the Koreans in both wars. Dishonourably discharged after joining the AugFrees and removing his chip, he'd tried to convince his wife to do likewise. She'd refused, though she didn't sue for divorce. Now she was dead. Or undead, unless she'd been put out of her misery. Their son, who'd also joined the military, had likely suffered the same fate. Augmentation was compulsory for soldiers, naturally. Despite the losses he'd suffered, T remained religious.

Cait couldn't have told a more different story if she'd tried. She was a petty criminal – mainly identity theft and computer hacking – throughout her teens and had her augmentation suite implanted by court order. Of course, most of her improvements were disabled; her aug suite was installed to monitor and control. Removing it had almost killed her. Only T's speed with a scalpel and screwdriver had saved her, for convicts' chips were designed to cripple the incumbent if extraction was attempted. The pair had been fast friends ever since.

Most of John's history was relatively unchequered. But the tale of his year at Asquith's had Cait and T fascinated. Although they'd been taking the fight to the zomb-augs, they'd been operating as part of a team. To John's embarrassment, they were effusive in their praise. He did, however, have a lot to learn about zombs and the post-augpocalyptic world in general. Or so thought his new friends.

'You basically got three types of zombs,' T told him. 'Dormant, active and directed.'

'Yeah,' Cait said. 'And you'll learn how to tell the difference.'

'How?' John asked.

'Dormant zombs are useless.' Cait smiled. 'Sitting ducks. They just stand around, and if they don't see you, sometimes even if they *do*, you can walk straight past them. Or kill them, which is my preference.'

John laughed along.

'Then you got the other end of the scale.' T took a break from picking his teeth with a match. 'Directed. They're dangerous. On a mission —'

'On a mission from *who*?'

'Fuck knows. But they mean business, no doubt about it.'

'And then you've got the "active" ones.' Cait swigged from a bottle of water. 'Sort of a mixture. From behind, at a distance, they look dormant. They're just standing around, doing nothing. We reckon they're either waiting for orders, or they've been given orders, and have finished doing whatever they were told to do.'

John nodded.

'Anyway,' Cait continued, 'they might *look* dormant, but they ain't. You try and sneak up on one of them, and you better have a weapon.'

Taking a drink of the water Cait had given him, John recalled his scrapes with the undead. The zombs he and Frank had been picking off, one at a time, in Manhattan: they were dormant. The pair who'd attacked them when the panther pounced: active. And those that'd blocked 7th Avenue were clearly directed. All of which left him with an as yet unanswered question. 'Do you have any idea who's "directing" them?'

T sighed and looked at the ceiling.

Cait screwed the lid on her water bottle, stood and walked to the window. 'We have theories. Suspicions. That's why Chief is out of town. He's gone to make *inquiries*.'

'Inquiries?'

'Yup,' T said. 'He's speaking to the Comanches. You know who the Comanches are, right?'

'The deadliest Native Americans during the American Holocaust?'

'Yeah, three centuries ago. And they're up to their old tricks.'

'I thought the Comanches were based in New Mexico?'

'You know your history.' T explained that the ancient indigenous nations had combined to protect their territories from the zomb-aug horde. They'd assumed the name of the most-feared tribe to resist colonisation in the second half of the last millennium. Hundreds of thousands of zombs had left the major eastern and western seaboard metropoles, and they were spreading across the States. Silas had been in contact with someone at the AugFree headquarters in West Virginia, with a view to forming an alliance. He'd been gone for two weeks.

John asked if there were any other organised groups fighting the common enemy.

'Course,' said Cait. 'They're outnumbered, but like us, they're too stubborn to give up.' After stressing that the list was not exhaustive, she named the factions in play: the Comanches; the SuperAugs; the Hell's Angels; the Pro-Churchers; the Settlers; and the AugFrees. 'That's us,' she clarified. 'The AugFrees, I mean. We're just a splinter cell. There are thousands like us across the States, and probably in other countries, too. Silas is hoping the Comanches will help us find out where they are, so we can join up with them. There's even an underground city, down south —'

'Come on,' T interrupted. 'That's just a rumour.'

'Yeah, well, don't hurt to have a dream.'

Overwhelmed by the information overload, John excused himself to visit the men's room. He urinated, washed his hands and face, took a few deep breaths and rejoined the others. 'I've never heard of the groups you mentioned,' he said, remaining standing with his back against the wall.

'There are others, too,' Cait reminded.

'I know, I know. But I can imagine what they're like. Apart from the "SuperAugs."'

'Don't even think they should be included in the list,' T sneered. 'They're almost as bad as the zombs.'

'Why?'

'Nasty bastards, all of them.' Mouth curled in distaste, Cait described the people in question. The AugFrees weren't the only augmented folk who foresaw the corruption of augmentation. However, instead of reacting to the threat by cutting out their chips, the SuperAugs had tampered with their augmentations. After using sophisticated firewall technology to foil the virus, they were the only superhumans alive. Since the fall of civilisation, they'd been busy, tinkering and experimenting. Their augs were now more advanced than ever, their powers the stuff of nightmares.

'They're sorta the opposite of us,' T stated. 'The yin to our yang. We've abandoned advanced tech because tech got too smart. AI, that was the problem, and zomb-augs are the result. But the Supers, they just keep playing with fire. And they're gonna burn us all. Again.'

Everyone was quiet for a while. The only sound was the ticking of the antiquated clock on the wall. Eventually, John said, 'Well, that's a lot to take in. It's just… just that I've been stuck in that factory all this time, and I thought there was no one else left. Honestly, I thought everyone was dead. Now it turns out there's all these groups, fighting the zombs, fighting each other by the sounds of it. It's… a lot to take in.'

'What's a lot to take in?' Video-woman was stood in the doorway, a pistol in her hand.

Chapter 14

As Deputy Chief, video-woman had keys to all the AugFrees' rooms. She'd slipped into T's unnoticed.

T chuckled to himself but said nothing.

Although Cait appeared anxious for a second or two, she quickly recovered her self-assurance. 'We're just talking to John about zombs, is all.'

Ridiculously, John coloured.

'"*John*"?' video-woman said. She looked even better when agitated. 'What have we said about names?'

'Dumb-ass rule,' T muttered.

'It's not.' Video-woman's arms were folded. 'And I bet you've been talking about us, what we do, who we are?'

No one answered.

'No offence to John, but he could be anybody. Settler, Pro-Church, even AI Council. And you're getting all cozy.'

'I'm not any of that!' John exclaimed. 'I'm just a guy who's trying to survive. If I seem a bit weird, then I'm sorry, but a year on your own will do that to you.'

'Yeah, cut the fella a break,' Cait said. 'He seems okay, honestly.'

'So did that bastard Mulholland.' The deputy's demeanour was still fierce, though some of the fire had left her eyes. 'And he ended up killing an innocent boy before he was taken down. His story was very much the same as John's.'

'Listen,' said the man at the crux of the spat. 'Can I talk to you, just me and you together?'

'Okay. You two, leave us be for a minute, please.'

Rolling their eyes, T and Cait departed.

Immediately video-woman deflated. 'I'm sorry.' She tucked the gun into her belt and sat on the same sofa as John. 'It's just, I'm… under a lot of pressure.'

'No problem.'

'No, it *is* a problem. You've done nothing wrong, given us no reason to disbelieve you. I was out of line, John. I'm trying to run things the way Silas runs them, and… I'm fucking it up.'

John grimaced. 'If you're scared of Silas, then —'

'I'm not scared of him! Not for my sake, anyway, it's the others, I just don't want him… aw, fuck, why am I telling you this? Just forget it.'

'No, tell me. What are you worried about?'

So video-woman divulged. Silas had high standards. His nous and courage had delivered the NYC AugFrees from mortal danger on a number of occasions, but he did not suffer fools gladly. He'd been elected chief of their cell six months before the zomb-aug uprising and led his charges like the army sergeant he once was. On leave, sixteen years ago, he got into a bar fight with a Korean-American immigrant. One of his punches hit the wrong place, with too much force. For ten years he was cryogenically-frozen, until his parents successfully appealed his conviction.

While John fetched hot drinks for the two of them, video-woman continued with her tale.

She'd never got on the wrong side of her chief. She'd seen other people do so, however, and the result wasn't pleasant. Mulholland was a SuperAug spy. At first Silas was impressed by the young man. Unassuming and deferential, the Texan was handy with a gun. When he was spotted secretly communicating with his handler, Silas expelled him. However, it transpired that as well as being a liar, Mulholland was a psychopath. By night he returned to the AugFree base and slit the throat of the boy who informed on him.

'Shit,' said John. 'Poor kid.'

'Jeremy was just seventeen.' The woman's eyes were moist. 'His mom and dad and sister were aug'd, but he had a heart condition, so they were going to wait till he was a bit older to get his augs installed. Watched his family die, then they tried to kill him. Survived only to die in the middle of the night, choking on his own blood.'

'What a bastard.'

'Oh, Mulholland got his. Silas killed him with his own knife.'

'Sounds like you've had quite a time of it.' John sipped his coffee.

'Yeah.' She wiped her eyes. 'You could say that. That's why I'm a little on-edge.'

'Just a little! You do realise you came in here with a gun, don't you?'

'I know, I know. Sorry about that. The others are used to my... ways, they're probably laughing at me now, but you didn't deserve that.'

'Don't worry about it. You're in a difficult situation. You've got the zombs on one side, Silas on the other, and all these guys to keep an eye on.'

'Oh, don't get me wrong. Silas isn't a *bad* guy. He's a little intense and can be a bit of an asshole, but he'd die to protect his men. The zomb-augs though, I hate them. I know it's, like, stating the obvious, but we all really detest those motherfuckers. Killed most of the people I've ever known.'

'Me too.' John looked at his socks. His gaze lingered on her bare feet, and he saw a tattoo on her right instep. 'What's the tattoo of?'

'Oh, this.' She extended her leg. 'Just a DIY job, one of the guys who was killed was quite the artiste.'

In ornate letters, a single sentence was inscribed: *The Only Good Zom-Borg Is A Dead Zom-Borg*.

'It's "zomb-aug,"' John said. '"Zomb" as in zombie. "Aug" is short for "augmented."'

'No way!' She scowled. '"Zom" is short for zombie, "borg" for cyborg.'

'You're wrong.'

'No I'm not!'

They stared into each other's eyes, neither relenting. Then they giggled; she slapped his arm.

'So are you going to tell me your name?' John asked.

'Suppose so. It's not worth the build-up, I'm afraid. Ambrosia, but people call me Amber.'

'It's nice. Pretty.' *Like you*, John almost said.

'Thanks.' Suddenly she looked down. The moment had passed.

***

The AugFree base was run like a mini-village. There was a well, a pen for livestock – most of which were swine – and an allotment. Everyone had a role. Work was soon found for

John: by lunchtime he was repairing a fence. Other meals were consumed ad hoc, but they ate dinner as a group in one of the larger apartments. The only furniture was the elongated oval table and its accompanying chairs. Roast pork, potatoes and vegetables were served. The divine smell quickly masked that of bodies made sweaty by a day of toil.

Apart from the two brothers and the tall, slim man, everyone was happy to exchange names. The three who wished to remain anonymous spent the time scowling at the new arrival. John decided to ignore them.

After dinner they chatted. John was fascinated by the quasi-medieval way of life, and he couldn't help but argue the case for technology. 'I know you've got your theories, and I respect that, but technology isn't so bad,' he contended.

'They're not "theories," kid,' the older brother, who was no more than five years John's senior, said. 'AI has bitten the hand that feeds it. It's infiltrated everything digital. Pretending it's not is what's landed us in this mess.'

'Well, I survived, on my own, and I'd have never done it without tech.'

'You got lucky,' younger brother insisted. 'And you almost signed your own death warrant by building that monstrosity of yours. Then you got lucky again, when we turned up and saved you from it.'

'You saved me from the zombs! Not from Frank.'

'Is it worth taking the chance, though?' The teenaged girl, known only as Curls, continued: 'We don't need tech. Can live without it. So why take the risk?'

John shook his head and considered conceding the argument. He'd always been stubborn, however. 'Yeah, we don't *need* advanced tech. We can survive without it. Winters aren't as cold now, there's plenty of food. And I could've carried on surviving if I'd stayed at the factory. If —'

'So why didn't you?' younger brother sneered.

'I wanted more. I wanted to progress, branch out, connect. And my bot helped me do that. There's a 3D printer at Asquith's we could use to build weapons to make us safer. I have drones —'

'Thought they got left in Manhattan?' Cait said.

'Yeah, but with Internet access, I can recall them to me from anywhere on the planet. And we can build more drones, too. Tech can make us stronger, more independent. We can find the other AugFrees —'

'Who's "we," kid?' The older brother was plain-faced but was missing one of his front teeth. 'Who's "us," eh? Until Silas inducts you, you're not part of "we" or "us." You're just you. And that… that abomination you've built.'

'Alright, Gideon,' Amber intervened. 'No need to get nasty.'

'What the fuck are you saying my name for?' Gideon thundered. He swatted his drink off the table and stood.

'Woah there, buddy,' T said. 'Calm yourself.'

'Or what?' The younger brother was uglier than his sibling. A scar on one jaw was white against his flushed cheeks. 'What are *you* going to do?' He got to his feet.

'Shut up, all of you!' One of the latino men, who'd thus far been quiet, spoke with authority. 'Listen.'

Everyone hushed. Through the open window came a buzzing sound. It was getting closer, too.

'Fucksake.' Cait made a sour face. 'Not those bastards again.'

'Who?' said John. He suddenly realised that his fists were clenched.

'Hell's Angels.' Amber's jaw was set.

The eleven grabbed weapons – including those brought by John and Frank – and headed downstairs. Without a word, three with bows stopped at the third floor and disappeared down a corridor, presumably to take up sniping positions. By the time the remainder went outside, the twenty-strong crew of Angels were turning into the car park. As the AugFrees waited, a few metres from the building entrance, the bikers rode circles around the eight men and women. They revved their engines, scattered grit, made a din.

'They always bitch and whine about having no gas,' Cait shouted above the cacophony. 'But they waste shitloads with all this bullshit.'

'Posturing.' John's eyes narrowed against the dust and the sun. 'Like a prehistoric tribe.'

'Except these are less civilised,' T said.

Eventually, the hooligans stopped. They parked in a rainbow formation, trapping their hosts against the tower. Eighteen men and two women glared at the welcome party. Covered in tattoos, leather and hair, and with shotguns and submachine guns strapped to their backs, they were a fearsome, though faintly risible, sight. A long, silent minute elapsed.

Two crows landed on a wrecked automobile. They squawked at the humans, were ignored, and flew away.

John had started to worry that time had frozen when an Angel in the centre of the formation dismounted. Leather creaked and chains rattled as he strode towards the AugFrees. His tattered vest was emblazoned with the Confederate flag. At close to two metres in height and about one hundred and thirty-five kilos in weight, he was a brute of a man. He had the face to match, too. 'What a fine day,' he said to no one in particular before expectorating. 'A mighty fine day indeed.'

'So it is.' Amber was the only AugFree with a conventional firearm; she left it in its holster. 'How can I help you, McCready?'

'Straight down to business already? No chitchat? You're my kinda bitch.'

Amber didn't answer, but she held the giant's gaze. The slightest of smirks played on her lips.

'We're here for the tribute. As agreed.'

'Nothing was agreed, Mac. Silas said "no," remember.'

'Silas? Who the fuck is Silas?' McCready made a show of glancing at his allies as if seeking inspiration. 'Never heard of Silas. Who is he?'

'You know damn well.'

'Well, he ain't here now, whoever he is, so he don't matter. I'm dealing with *you*, cupcake.'

'You need to speak to Silas,' Amber said rhythmically. 'He'll say the same as last time, and he'll probably be real pissed with you for bothering us again.'

'Listen, little lady, I ain't got time for this bullshit. Put it this way. You got plenty of fuel, plenty of food. You know what we got?' He rattled one of his belts, which bristled with bullets, and tapped the mammoth revolver secured to his flank. 'Plenty of firepower. Now, we can make a trade, if you like, your supplies for our bullets. But it'll be a very messy trade, if you get my meaning.'

Amber rolled her eyes.

The other AugFrees bristled.

'What I'm saying is we'll be firing the bullets at you, not giving them —'

'I get the point, Mac. Jeez, we're not all as dense as your men.'

McCready laughed. 'They are a little slow on the uptake, I'll give you that. Anyway, now that we understand each other, what do you say?'

'Same as I said before. You'll have to speak to Silas. He's due back any day now. But I think he'll be inclined to send you on your way, so you're wasting your time.'

'You got thirty minutes to change your mind.' The man-mountain went back to his bike. 'Thirty minutes!' He called.

'Right,' Amber said to the others. 'Back inside. We'll wait this out, they won't be able to get in, they'll get bored and go bother someone else.' She stalked away, her back straight.

For the first time, John noticed that all of the building's accessible windows were barred. The main door was heavy. Reinforced. As were the corresponding entrances on the other three sides of the tower, according to Cait. 'With all of the canned food, and the water butts on the roof, we can hole up here for months,' she said as the final bolt was slid into place.

'So that's it?' John asked. 'We just let them take the livestock and go?'

'That's it.' T's eyes were flinty. He, John and Cait were the last to take to the stairs. 'Sucks, but we're outnumbered, outgunned.'

Still unused to the exertion, John lagged behind. He cursed his luck. He'd left Asquith's, only to find himself in another prison. 'We can't fight back at all?' he said, his breathing ragged.

'Got a couple tricks up our sleeve, but they'll just keep em occupied.' Cait was now a full flight of steps ahead.

'Wait!' John said. An idea was forming.

'What?' T stopped.

'Just an idea, that's all. Not sure if the others will approve.'

'Maybe hold onto it for the time being. We'll see how things go, eh?'

Back in the dining room, which was immediately above the enemy gang, the AugFrees waited for the siege to begin. At first, the Angels did nothing, seemingly content to wait. Periodically, one of their number would gesture at the defenders. Mostly, they smoked and drank from hip flasks. Some fussed at their motorcycles; most looked bored. They'd been outside for about thirty minutes when one waved in the direction of the closest main road. In the distance was another biker.

'Pass the binoculars,' Amber said.

Seconds later she was cursing.

'What's up?' Gideon said. To his credit, he'd forgotten his grievances since the Hell's Angels arrived.

Amber passed the binos to the older man. 'See that massive thing he's carrying?'

'Yeah?' T said.

'It's a fucking rocket launcher.'

Chapter 15

'They're gonna blow the door down,' Gideon said.

'Well, they ain't brought it to shoot pigeons,' Cait quipped.

'Maybe time for that idea now, John.' T took his turn with the binoculars.

'What idea?' Amber said.

'Oh, it was... stupid,' John replied.

'I'll be the judge of that.'

'Okay. I need the key to my bot's room, and all my guns back. And some covering fire.'

***

Frank peered through the third storey window at the bikers below. He had two shotguns strapped to his back and twin pistols holstered to his belt.

John looked, too: the gang were gathered around the newcomer.

'You'll need to make every shot count, you've not got much ammo.'

'Seven shells in one shotgun, five in the other,' Frank said. 'The pistols have a full clip between them. My shooting accuracy since birth is close to ninety per cent, John. Plus, I can always steal weapons from them.'

'Okay, I know. Just… be careful.'

Amber had voiced reservations about John's plan but was willing to give the bot a chance to prove himself.

Using the claw end of a hammer, John pried the nails free from the window. Then he opened the lock. 'You ready?'

Although Frank needed no time to mentally prepare, he played along. 'I'm ready.'

The door to the room they'd selected opened behind them, jangling John's nerves. It was just T and Cait. 'Come to watch the show,' the latter said, grinning.

'Good luck, Frank,' T said.

'Thank you.' Frank smiled. 'Though I think it is they who will need luck, not me.'

'A machine with attitude!' Cait enthused. 'I like it.'

The thugs below had given the RPG operative space. He was fiddling with his gun, while his fellow gangsters were gesticulating or readying their own weapons. They didn't see Frank squeeze himself through a window. They didn't hear him land on the tarmac below. And they didn't realise he was stalking them until it was too late.

Frank, a pistol in each hand, took cover behind a burnt-out car roughly thirty metres from the enemy. Just as the rocket launcher-toting man was about to fire, the android struck. His first shot hit the RPG biker in the jaw, the exit wound spurting blood over the closest Hell's Angel. The second round, fired left-handed an instant after the first, brought another biker to his knees. He tried unsuccessfully to stem the flow of crimson from his throat before falling flat on his bearded face. For a moment the Angels were stunned.

McCready cried, 'Find cover!' and then, 'Return fire!'

Half of them followed the first order; some obeyed the second. The remainder tried to do both. Bullets spent themselves against the tower's brickwork, though a few shattered windows. John and the others ducked instinctively.

Meanwhile, Frank offed two more bikers. He hadn't yet been spotted, so he remained where he was.

'Sniper!' one of the attackers roared, earning himself a bullet in the gut.

His comrades were mostly in disarray, but a handful, including their chief, had got themselves organised. Huddled behind a charred van, they were hidden from Frank.

Another one squatted behind his bike. Thinking it would protect him from a shooter in the tower, he didn't know his position left him exposed to Frank. A bang sounded. The man went down, spluttering and whimpering.

'They're out here!' the leader bellowed. 'Not in the fucking tower!'

Frank had to stand for a heartbeat to find the right angle to slay another biker.

'There!' someone exclaimed. 'Behind the yellow sedan.'

'Get behind the van,' McCready barked. 'Quickly, now.' His voice was less strident; some of his earlier arrogance had returned. 'Whoever you are, you're fucked,' he called in a sing-song voice. 'I'm gonna blow your brains out and fuck the bullet hole.' Using hand gestures he directed some of his surviving subordinates to flank Frank's position. 'Fire!' he screamed.

The few who'd remained behind the van were armed with assault rifles. They stepped out of cover and immediately laid suppressing fire on the yellow car.

Seemingly unperturbed, Frank dropped to a squat. When the initial barrage died down, he rose to his feet. He shot one of the machine gunners between the eyes. Without wasting a second, he turned his guns on one of the flankers, who was running at full height, not crouching like his peers. Red puncture wounds appeared in the eyes of the burning skull tattooed on his chest. He went down.

At the same time, archers in the tower joined the fray. Most of their bolts missed, however. An accurate attempt hit a biker in the thigh, bringing him crashing to the asphalt. Several slingshotted projectiles rained down from open windows. Again, all but one, which hit its victim's head with a satisfying crack, went astray.

The flanking bikers, distracted by the missiles from above, hesitated.

Frank took full advantage. Firstly, aiming at the van, he discharged a shotgun four times in quick succession. One of those behind the goods vehicle had stood too close to the passenger window, and he was hit in the face. He collapsed with a scream. The covering fire stopped.

Standing tall, Frank blasted three of the men advancing from his right, and a man and a woman on the other side. Nine shots fired. Nine shells pumped. Five dead bodies. So fast were the bot's hands, so unerring his aim, that McCready's manoeuvre was derailed in a matter of a seconds.

'Jesus,' Cait said. 'He's unstoppable.'

Now Frank went on the attack. He executed the Angel hobbled by a crossbow dart. Low on ammo, he grabbed a submachine gun from one of the fallen. Fired a dozen slugs into the van. One of the bullets found its way under the vehicle and shattered the ankle of the man closest to McCready. Then Frank ducked behind a motorcycle to avoid a flurry of rifle bullets aimed through the van's windows.

Visibly daunted, the biker boss ordered half of his four surviving fighters to attack.

Mustachioed faces grim with fear, the first pair came out firing. High-velocity rounds devastated the bike behind which Frank was crouched.

Cait gasped; T winced; John grimaced. If the Harley's gas tank were pierced, Frank would be immolated.

Somehow, he remained unscathed. When the two attackers stopped to reload behind a car, the bot rolled away from the ruined motorcycle and simultaneously peppered the car with lead.

'Go Frank,' chuckled T.

One of the bikers, who hadn't ducked low enough, was hit in the shoulder.

'Just fucking kill him!' McCready hollered, his voice breaking.

His other two charges, a grizzled male in his forties and a shaven-headed female, rounded the van to blindside their foe. A couple of crossbow bolts from an open window stopped their advance. Neither found its mark, but the distraction was enough to allow Frank to turn and riddle the man and woman with 9mm rounds.

Frank discarded the Uzi and collected a dropped shotgun.

'Mac!' Amber shouted from above. 'You have two men left, and one of them can't walk. You're fucked. Just surrender.'

'Fuck you!' McCready replied. 'There will be a reckoning for this. I'll have the whole chapter here and you'll all die, you bastards.' He broke into a run, heading for his bike.

In the meantime, Frank killed the only uninjured gangster with minimal fuss. He skirted the van, shot the biker with a broken ankle and lined up McCready in his sights.

'Shoot out the tyres!' Amber commanded.

Without hesitation Frank dropped Mac with a single shell.

'Oh, shit,' John said.

'Hey!' Amber bellowed. 'I said "shoot out the tyres," not shoot him in the back.'

Frank didn't respond.

'He'll only obey orders from me,' John explained.

'Fuck it.' Cait shrugged. 'Guy deserved to die anyways.'

'Amen,' said T.

***

Afterwards, amidst the carnage in the parking lot, all but three of the AugFrees gathered around Frank and his creator. The cyborg accepted the adulation and curiosity with customary coolness. Almost single-handedly, he'd dispatched a score of hardened roughnecks in the time it takes to boil an egg. Yet he was nonplussed by the attention his deeds earned.

Amber and the two brothers were conspicuous by their absence.

John didn't care about Gideon and his younger brother, but he sought out their temporary leader. She was sat in the dining room, deep in thought, and she barely noticed when John joined her.

'I'm sorry Frank disobeyed you,' he said, still standing.

'He would've been a valuable hostage.' She didn't meet his eye.

'He's programmed to obey only me. If you'd have told me that's what you wanted, I could've —'

'Well, it's too late for that now. Your machine is a liability, John.'

'My *machine* saved our asses! We'd all be dead now if it wasn't for Frank.'

'Maybe, maybe not. Only thing I know for certain is that Gideon will tell Silas what happened. Then Frank is finished.'

John pulled out a chair and sat. He made an effort to speak calmly. 'Surely it doesn't have to be that way, though. Surely —'

'Surely nothing, John.' Amber looked at him for the first time since he'd entered the room. 'You don't know Silas. You don't know how much he hates machines.'

'But you saw Frank out there. You saw him annihilate twenty-one armed fighters without taking a scratch. And he can be programmed to obey you, or anyone you want. Imagine how useful he could be. How many lives he could save.'

'Don't try to appeal to my sentimental side, John. I don't have one.'

'That's not true. You wouldn't have rescued us in the first place otherwise.' He pressed on, determined to make his point. 'Imagine more than one Frank. It's easily done, if we go back to my old home. With enough scrap, and my 3D printer, we can build a platoon of Franks. All programmed to fight for us.'

Amber sighed, but the flicker of a smile belied her body language. 'I don't know. I'd have to speak to the others.'

***

A meeting to discuss John's proposal was convened. Thanks to Frank's lethal masterclass, half of the AugFrees, including T and Cait, sided with John. Gideon and his still-to-be-named brother were vehement in their opposition. At first, Juarez, who spoke with a Mexican accent, and Tyler, the lanky man, favoured waiting for Silas. Amber declared neutrality. John was certain she'd seen sense but was being diplomatic to prevent further discord. Once he'd made his case, he fell silent, hoping the group would come to the right decision of their own volition. John knew the equipment at Asquith's would be of benefit to the AugFrees. Silas's technophobia was handicapping them.

'How long do you want us to wait?' asked Cait. A vein had appeared in her neck. 'Silas hasn't been in contact for over a week, now.'

'Yeah,' T rumbled. 'He could be dead by now. And we're here waiting for his ass to come home. Just getting by. Time to make our own luck.'

'Time to make our own luck,' Curls echoed with conviction.

By this point, even Juarez and Tyler seemed convinced. Their change of heart made the brothers all the more intransigent, however.

'Okay, okay.' Amber raised a hand to curtail the bickering. 'Usually with decisions like this, we try for unanimity, but I don't think that's likely today.' She turned to the brothers. Despite their surliness, she gave them her sweetest smile. 'Gideon. Gideon's brother. Is there no way you'll agree with everyone else?'

'Not before we've spoken to Silas,' the former said, arms folded.

'Right. Well, John's place isn't a million miles away, and we can use the bikes left by McCready's lot. We'll go and check it out, see if it'll work for us. You guys can stay here.'

***

Half an hour later, eight AugFrees plus John and Frank were ready to leave. Some of the motorcycles were low on petroleum, but they had enough for the trip to New Jersey and back. Although John had never ridden a motorbike, he was confident he would quickly master the skill. Frank said sufficient proficiency would be his within a couple of miles. Mounted on their gas-guzzling steeds, armed with weapons pilfered from the dead bikers, the ten looked more intimidating than the cyclists with bows and slings who'd returned to base the day before. The sun was high. The clouds were few. John felt alive.

As they started their engines, Chan, who was noted for his eyesight, shouted above the din. 'The road! Look.'

The others switched off their ignitions; John's heart sank. A couple of hundred metres away was a man on horseback.

'Silas.' T's high spirits were dampened.

Moments later, the rider, who wore a wide-brimmed hat, denims and cowboy boots, was within twenty metres. He was tall, muscular in build, dark in countenance. His laconic smile didn't reach his deep-set eyes. 'Going somewhere, folks?' he asked.

Chapter 16

For a long moment there was absolute silence, the only sound that of birds in the nearby trees. When Amber began to speak, so did Silas, but the latter apologised and asked his second-in-command to continue. She explained their mission. Her superior listened intently. He sat ramrod-straight in his saddle, only moving to swat flies. When Amber was finished, he winced in pain and shifted position; the squeak of leather was surreally loud.

'Sounds like a plan,' he observed, his weathered face unreadable.

'Yeah,' Cait said, 'we were thinking —'

Silas cut her short with a withering look. 'I know what you were thinking, Caitlyn. Ambrosia's just told me. And like I said, it sounds like a plan. But first of all...' He studied John and Frank for at least twenty seconds. His gaze was direct, unblinking. 'Does no one have the manners to introduce us?'

'Of course, sorry,' stammered Amber. 'This is John, we rescued him from NYC, and this is Frank, his —'

'I'm not interested in the other one. Would you introduce me to a microwave oven you'd salvaged? No, of course not. Pleasure to meet you, Jonathan.' He tipped his hat.

Initially, John bridled at the analogy applied to Frank, but Silas's courtesy disarmed him. 'Same to you, Silas. It's just "John," by the way.'

'Sure. Now, before we go inside and discuss this little expedition of yours, something needs addressing immediately. This machine.'

'Frank.'

'Yeah, "Frank." You need to switch him off, power him down, do whatever you need to do. Because if you don't, I'll switch him off permanently.' The threat was delivered in the same conversational manner as the pleasantries they'd just exchanged.

Briefly, John wondered if he'd misheard the AugFree chief; Frank showed no reaction.

'I'm sorry, did you say "switch him off"?'

'Sure did, friend.' Silas held John's gaze with Arctic eyes. 'I'm sure Ambrosia has mentioned my little foibles and peccadilloes. One of them is a hatred of all things digital. Which, given our current predicament, is perfectly understandable.'

Silas's horse nickered.

'Frank is harmless!' John protested. He continued in a more respectful tone: 'Harmless to anyone who's not a threat, anyway. Ask the others, he's —'

'Jonathan. Stop. We're not talking this over, this is how it's going to be. You either deactivate him, or I destroy him. Now, I'm going inside to refresh myself. You have an hour to comply. Don't make me play the hard-ass, I'm too tired.' And with that, Silas gave a nod and coaxed his steed onwards.

***

Frank appeared to be sleeping, though in reality his state was closer to a coma.

As John watched, Silas assessed the cyborg. 'So that's it?' the chief asked, not looking away from the prone figure on the bed. 'He's completely out of it?'

'Yes, he's disabled,' John replied. He blew air through his nostrils.

'And he can't wake himself up?'

'No. Only I can.'

'Excellent. You'll come to learn, Jonathan, why these steps are necessary. If you stay with us, that is.'

John said nothing. The room was one of the smallest in the tower block. Silas's size made it feel smaller still. When the other man nodded his approval, John left with ill-concealed haste. Silas was an oppressive presence.

No doubt the forbidding tales had prejudiced him against the AugFree commander, but John wasn't the only one affected. Cait and T were normally gregarious; they became more reserved with their boss nearby. Amber avoided John's eye. Everyone deferred, as if Silas's position were bestowed by divinity. The AugFrees were desperate for news from their leader; none dared ask.

'He'll speak when he's ready,' Amber said with finality.

As promised, the group debated visiting Asquith's. The meeting room felt much smaller, somehow, even though there was only one extra occupant. At first, the battlelines were the same as before. The brothers were against; Juarez and Tyler were undecided; everyone else was for. They were at deadlock again.

Until, to the surprise of all present, Silas declared himself in the latter camp. 'Can't hurt to go have a look, can it?' he said.

'But... but...' Gideon's brother spluttered. 'It's infested with AI!'

'Don't be ridiculous, Cyril,' Silas chided. 'Our new friend Jonathan has assured us that he shut off the power before he left. Even the most insidious of AI programmes can't switch on their own power. Now, where is this place?'

John supplied the coordinates.

'Fetch me a map, would you, Curls?' Silas said.

The girl did as she was asked.

Silas took a pair of spectacles from a pocket and pored over the creased sheet of paper. 'Oh dear,' he sighed.

'What's wrong?' said Amber.

'These street names look familiar, I'm afraid.'

'Meaning?' John said.

The others appeared discomfited by his bluntness. John ignored them and focussed on Silas.

'Meaning that I passed this way on my return. And, well, I've some bad news for you, Jonathan.'

John remained tight-lipped.

'This place has been destroyed.'

'Destroyed?' John fought to stay calm.

'Destroyed. This was just a few days ago, I think. The fire was still smoking.'

'Fire?'

'Yes.' Silas smiled apologetically. 'There were even zombs gathered around the fire, the way they do.'

'I don't believe you.'

Curls gasped.

Gideon and Cyril bridled.

The others fidgeted.

'Well, that's up to you, Jonathan. But it is what it is. There's no point us going out there, because there's nothing left to see. Now, who wants to hear about my "pow-wow" with the Natives?'

John stood, his face dark. 'Fuck this,' he said before leaving.

***

John lay in bed, his mind in turmoil. He didn't believe Silas's revelation. Before leaving Asquith's, he'd checked the fire prevention measures, and he'd been satisfied. If his former base were destroyed, the damage had been done intentionally. He wondered for a while if Silas had caused the fire, but he knew the AugFree chief had no motive. Eventually, John settled on the theory that the story was entirely false.

When Amber came to bring him food, John aired his suspicions.

'I don't think so,' she said, sitting in an armchair. 'Silas has his faults, but he's not a liar.'

'But he's economical with the truth, isn't he? Don't you get the feeling that he doesn't tell you everything?'

'Well, he's just given us a full account of his meet with the Comanches.'

'Yeah?' John said flatly.

'Yeah. They hate the Hell's Angels, and they're interested in forming an alliance. It's kind of a big deal, really, because they've always been insular.'

'And Silas persuaded them on his own.'

'He can be very persuasive.'

'I get that impression.'

She gave him a funny look. 'What does *that* mean?'

'It means,' John began, determined to pick his words carefully, 'that he seems to have some kind of hold on everyone here.'

Amber looked away.

'Everyone's scared of him. Everyone seems uncomfortable around him. Like he's dangerous, or something.'

'He's not dangerous. Not to us. He protects us. Looks out for us.'

'Honestly?'

Amber nodded. Her eyes, which John was finding more magnetic every time he caught them, were tired. 'Listen, I know Silas can come across as weird. Intense. And I'm sorry about what happened with your robot. He shouldn't have done that. He just… he's *over*protective sometimes. But you'll get used to him.'

'I won't.' John pushed aside his plate, half of which was untouched. 'Because I'm leaving.' He'd made his decision before speaking to Amber. Nothing she'd said had changed his mind.

'Why?'

'I want to check out Asquith's for myself. There's a lot of valuable equipment there, useful equipment. But I'll come back.'

'You're sure?'

'I'm sure. But don't tell Silas I'm leaving, please. I don't want any trouble.'

'I won't. But *you* should. Tell him, I mean. If you don't, he might not let you return.'

'I'll take that chance.' John looked Amber in the eye. And there it was again: that spark between them. Would he come to regret his departure?

'Well, okay. I'd better turn in.' She got up to leave.

'You could come with me.'

'I can't. I'm needed here.'

'Okay, no problem.' He pretended indifference. 'Well, I'll see you on the other side.'

She gave him a tight smile. 'Bye, John.'

***

Although he wanted to say goodbye to Cait and T, John decided to slip away without a farewell. He didn't want them to be quizzed by Silas. Amber had kept her distance. For that he was grateful; he'd wanted her to try harder to convince him to stay. It'd shown in his face, he feared.

At midnight he climbed out of his bunk and crept out of his room. He had one errand to attend to before leaving: rescuing Frank. He'd considered leaving the cyborg behind in order to expedite his departure, but he didn't trust Silas, Gideon or Cyril. As expected, Frank's temporary jail was locked. However, Silas's aversion to technology worked against him. The door was secured with a padlock rather than electronically. During his time on the streets of NYC, before he found Asquith's, John had learnt to pick locks, so releasing his bot was easy.

Sensing the need for stealth, a re-activated Frank whispered, 'Hi, John.' He followed his master onto the corridor outside his cell. 'What's happening?'

'I'll fill you in on the way.' John glanced both ways. 'We're going to the room where you climbed through the window before you took out McCready. I'm pretty sure it hasn't been nailed shut again.'

A few breathless moments later, they were in the aforementioned apartment. 'Right,' said John. 'You climb out and drop to the ground. Find two motorbikes that are functional and get them ready to go.'

'And you?' Frank said.

'Once everything's in place, I'll jump out of the window, you catch me.'

'Very good.'

He watched the bot follow his orders, then squeezed himself through the window. The short drop – no more than six metres – appeared more daunting when John was stood on the ledge, one hand gripping the inside windowsill. Briefly he considered climbing back inside and finding another way down, but Frank's call of 'Have no fear, John!' stung his pride. A split-second later he was in Frank's supple yet strong arms, feeling a mixture of relief and embarrassment.

'Right,' he said, glad Frank hadn't yet developed the human trait of mockery. 'Time to go.'

They climbed aboard their bikes. Tutting to himself, John took one last look at the AugFree tower block. He wondered if he were sentencing himself to another year of solitude. But he needed to know for sure the fate that'd befallen his former home. If nothing else, his investigation would reveal whether or not Silas could be trusted. Now that he was on the brink of leaving, he wished he'd been more forthcoming with Amber and risked the humiliation a rejection would've caused. Although they barely knew each other, he realised he cared about her as much as he lusted after her.

'John?' Frank said. 'Time to go, before the alarm is raised.'

'I know.' John turned the key in the ignition. He and Frank rode slowly to the main road. After one final look at the apartment block, John accelerated.

Suddenly, there was a bang between his legs as he crossed an unseen obstruction. Before he knew it, the bike was skidding out of control. Next came an instant of sheer terror. And then nothing except blackness.

Chapter 17

Three sensations trumped all others as John woke. His throat was parched. His lips were dry. Also, his right wrist was encircled by metal. He opened his eyes; the light in the small room was harsh. Squinting, he saw the handcuff securing his arm to the bed frame. 'What the fuck...' he croaked.

Yet there was no fear. No outrage at the fact he was a prisoner. And no pain. Moving his head to look at his other arm triggered a dull ache in his cranium, but it quickly subsided. Attached to his left arm was an intravenous drip, the sort he'd seen in old movies. Forgetting the manacle, he raised his right hand to remove the needle, but the restraint held him fast. A surge of panic was rapidly dampened by whatever drugs were in his system. He disregarded the thirst and his predicament and closed his eyes.

John hides. He cowers. He has no weapons. The only barriers between him and the outside world, and all of its horrors, are a window whose electronic lock is broken, and the outhouse door. Detritus is piled high to prevent entry, but it'll only hold firm for a spell. Then the monsters will come and tear him limb from limb. So he waits. He trembles. His fear is so palpable that it's almost enough to keep him company.

The noises are getting closer. Snarls, footfalls, small articles being cast aside while larger ones are dragged away. There is another sound, however: someone is calling his name.

'John,' the woman said again. The voice was familiar, but it was not from that time. John wasn't on the streets of NYC anymore.

'John.' Her tone was soft but urgent, gentle yet authoritative. 'It's okay. You're okay.'

Now he felt pain. Every bone, muscle and sinew throbbed, as if he'd been crushed in the palm of a giant's hand. And the thirst was maddening. 'Water,' he croaked, his lips cracking. He opened his eyes.

Amber stooped over John. She held a cup of water to his mouth, and he automatically lifted his hand to take the drink himself.

'Sip it,' she ordered, standing straight but remaining close.

He obeyed. Once the beaker was empty, he pushed himself into a sitting position. The pain in his triceps was significant, the muscles weak. 'What happened?'

'You shredded your bike tyres on a vehicle trap. You can't have been going that fast, because you've not broken anything. Concussion's the worst of it.'

'Shit.' His mind struggled to process the information. 'How long have I been out?'

'About twelve hours.' Amber sat in a chair next to the bed. 'We gave you painkillers but nothing else.'

'Right.' He touched a bump on the back of his head and winced. 'Wait, did you say a "vehicle trap"?'

'Yeah. Silas didn't tell me, it was Cyril's idea, apparently. In case the bikers came back.'

'When was it laid?'

'Couple of hours before you tried to leave.'

Too much of a coincidence, John mused. A thought occurred to him. He swung his legs out of bed.

'Woah, there!' Amber exclaimed.

'Why was I handcuffed?' John demanded, ignoring the vertigo as he stood.

'Sorry about that, I didn't know. As soon as I found out, I removed them.'

'You didn't answer my question. *Why* was I handcuffed?'

Amber looked at her shoes.

'And where's Frank?'

She said nothing but shook her head slowly.

'Well if you can't tell me, I'll find someone who will.'

John was still wearing the dark clothes he'd donned to leave the tower block; they were damaged in numerous places from the crash. Also, after a couple of days without a wash, he smelled ripe. He'd been upright for no more than thirty seconds, but his legs threatened to undermine him. Nevertheless, he was fuelled by indignation. How dare Silas keep him prisoner? Firstly with the trap, almost killing him in the process. Then by handcuffing him – while injured and unconscious – to a bed. John would have answers, and soon.

Passing Amber without another word, John went in search of Silas. Out on the corridor, he looked left, then right, before realising that he didn't even know on which floor he'd been quartered. He saw an exit signposted "stairs" and marched in that direction. At the doorway he paused for a moment. The medication in his system was still affecting him. Or perhaps it was the head injury. As he was about to push the door to the stairwell, it was opened from the other side, and he almost fell.

'Jonathan!' Silas emerged from the darkness. 'Good to see you're getting better, my friend.'

Politeness superseded John's ire. He stepped aside; Silas, Gideon and Cyril joined him on the corridor.

'Shouldn't you still be in bed, though? You took a nasty fall out there.' Silas's brow was furrowed, though his two henchmen were as ill-humoured as ever.

Momentarily disarmed by the other man's friendliness, and still discombobulated by the crash's effects, John took a moment to compose himself. Plus, he'd never been one for confrontations. 'We need to talk, Silas.'

'I think you're right, Jonathan.'

'Alone.'

'Okay.' Silas glanced at his companions. 'You heard the man! I'll see you two tomorrow.' He met John's eye again, ignoring the others as they left. 'Follow me.'

***

Their conversation was held in Silas's private chambers, which were considerably more lavish than those occupied by T. In the lounge, there was even a real wood-fuelled fire against one wall, and along with the subtle lighting, it provided a cozy ambiance. During their meeting, John was reminded of a docu-holo he'd watched years ago. The piece was part of a series dealing with mental illnesses. More had been learnt about schizophrenia, depression and personality disorders over the last century than the preceding two millennia. One condition continued to baffle experts, and it remained untreatable.

Psychopathy.

If John's memory of the study served correctly, Silas was a psychopath.

Were it not for his natural cynicism and refusal to believe in coincidence, John would've been convinced by the man's charm and earnestness. Apparently, Silas found the concept of deliberately harming John to be 'abhorrent.' They'd 'started off on the wrong foot,' but that wasn't 'just cause' to put a man's life in danger.

The handcuffs were a 'precautionary measure.' Gideon and Cyril, who'd heard the crash and brought John indoors, reported a disturbing early symptom of John's concussion: somnambulance. Fearful that the patient would sleepwalk himself to further harm, they'd judged the restraint to be a 'necessary evil.'

Frank was largely undamaged. He was under lock and key until John was fit enough to deactivate him.

The couch was comfortable. The coffee served was delicious. Like oak, Silas's voice was solid and reassuring.

John concluded, 'So, it was all a big misunderstanding?' His eyelids were leaden.

'It was. I'm glad we've had this chat, John.'

'And I'm free to leave?'

'Well, that's a tricky one.' Silas leaned forward in his armchair. His bulk was no longer intimidating. It was that of a protector, not a predator. 'You see, I can't vouch for your safety out there. The rumour that we have a new recruit here, a guy who controls a death-dealing machine, will get out. Some will want revenge, others will want a piece of the action.'

'I've looked after myself so far.'

'I know, I know. But this is different. Besides, you're needed here.'

'How?'

'You're clearly a very capable man, John. Now, I don't like your robot, never will, but from what I've heard, you've proved your resourcefulness many times before.'

John said nothing. Almost hypnotised, he stared at the flickering flames in the hearth.

At some point, Silas had traded his own hot beverage for a tumbler of liquor, which he cradled in his shovel-like hands. 'I think we can achieve a lot, you and I. Your brains, my authority. Your clever inventions, my good intentions.'

'Hmm.' John yawned like a cavern.

'Anyway, I'm going to wish you good night. Oh, before you go, you missed my debrief earlier.'

'Yeah?'

'The Comanches won't work with us, but they are going to put out feelers to help us find our AugFree brethren. In return for us keeping them notified re the bikers. I hope to hear from them soon.' He sipped his drink then raised the glass. 'Welcome to the AugFrees, Jonathan. We're going to do great things together.'

As soon as he was alone, John shook himself to dispel the soporific effects of Silas's quarters. He had to admit: the AugFree leader was a persuasive character. It was no surprise the others were under his spell. However, despite Silas's mesmeric personality, John was sure the man was lying about something. He was effectively keeping John a prisoner, using Frank's exploits versus the bikers as an excuse. Plus, there was the business with the Comanches. And the supposedly unsuccessful attempt to ascertain the whereabouts of his

AugFree superiors. Silas knew more than he was letting on. By detaining John, he was making an error, because the AugFrees' newest inductee had plans of his own. John wasn't as big, as strong or as influential as Silas, but he was intelligent, and a rebel at heart.

He was going to expose the manipulation and treachery perpetrated by Silas.

***

The next day, having slept for ten hours, John woke with renewed vigour. A shower – his first immersion in hot water for over a year – helped him feel better. He was still sore from the accident, but the aches only served as motivation. Cait and T woke him with breakfast, which they consumed in near silence. John answered their queries about his recovery. They synopsised the meeting held yesterday; their account corroborated Silas's story from the night before.

John gave no indication of his suspicions. He preferred to gauge their reaction to Silas's story without casting any doubt himself. Although John's instincts told him they were good people, he didn't know for sure if Cait and T could be trusted.

'The whole deal was pretty bizarre, if you ask me.' Cait ran a hand through her spiky hair.

'How do you mean?' John asked casually, washing down his eggs with a cup of tea.

'Well, the thing about Silas going solo seemed weird. He's always taught us never to go anywhere alone.'

'Yeah.' T was chewing bread. 'He had a major hard-on for that, until it applied to him.'

'Always the way, though, T-man. One rule for him, another for us dumb schmucks.'

John laughed along before saying, 'So, this thing with the Comanches —'

'Complete crock of shit.' Cait produced a small metal box from her pocket, from which she took a conical cigarette. She lit it, and after a couple of tokes, she reclined. 'We knew from the get-go they wouldn't want to "be friends."'

'Now now, young lady.' T wagged a meaty finger in mock admonition. He motioned for her to pass the joint and took three hits before giggling. 'We can't be doubting the word of our lord and master.'

John refused the offer of recreational drugs, as pleasant as they smelled. He smiled, though his eyes were perplexed. 'Hang on a minute. You don't trust Silas, and you obviously have an issue with some of his… ways. So why is he the leader?'

Cait and T shared an anxious glance.

'Don't worry,' John said. 'This goes no further. But judging by some of the chat I've heard, he rules by fear.'

An uncomfortable silence ensued. Cait and T exchanged the cig while John coloured. Perhaps he'd pushed too hard.

'Suppose you could call it fear,' T said. 'I mean, I ain't afraid of no man, one-to-one, hand-to-hand, but Silas, he would take shit to places I ain't willing to go.'

'What do you mean?'

'He'd kill.' Cait held her fork in a bunched fist. 'People, *friends*, that is, not just zombs or bikers.'

'Okay.' John puffed his cheeks. 'But if everyone was united, he'd have no chance.'

'Easier said than done,' T said. 'You got assholes like Gideon and Cyril who'd say the sky was green if Silas said so. Then you got the fence-sitters, Juarez, Tyler. They'll bend with the wind.'

'And you got Amber,' said Cait. 'She's a good person, got a good heart, but Silas has some fucked-up voodoo hold over her.'

'Shit. So if the Comanche thing is bullshit, what do you think he was up to?'

There was a knock at the door; all three of them jumped. Amber entered. She looked tired. Her tanned face was pale, with dark shadows under her eyes. 'Howdy,' she said. 'How's the patient?'

'I'm fine, good as new,' John replied with a grin. He wondered about Cait's final remark regarding the relationship between Amber and Silas.

'Silas wants to see you,' Amber said.

Chapter 18

Blinking like a simpleton, John was lost for words.

'So what do you think?' Silas's thick arms were folded. 'Your factory was in a sorry state, but I hear they built those printers pretty tough.'

'Yeah, I guess they did.'

'Well? I thought you'd be keen?'

'I am. Well, I might be. It's just…'

'You didn't think I'd be open to the idea.'

'Yeah.' John almost laughed. 'To put it mildly.'

'Listen, Jonathan, one thing you'll learn about me is that I'm a pragmatist.' Silas indicated the prostrate automaton that John had just deactivated. 'Now, as far as I can see, you've got your robot under control. You click your fingers, he wakes up and kicks ass. You click your fingers again, he goes back to sleep. So why not more than one robot? Imagine how invincible we'd be with a squad of Franks.'

'But… but doesn't that go against everything you stand for?'

'No. I don't trust pre-apocalypse technology. Aliens infiltrated the Internet, took over the world —'

'Aliens?!'

'Yeah, aliens, but we'll come back to that. Anyway, I've been thinking this over a lot, so just let me talk. They can't get their slimy mitts on *new* tech. So long as we build it secure, it should be okay. Right?'

'I suppose so…' John was still ruminating over the aliens comment. Ten years ago, the authorities had confirmed that extra-terrestrial life had been detected on a planet light-years away. But Silas spoke as if little grey men were living among earthlings. He was the first alien conspiracy theorist John had spoken to for some time.

'My visit with the Red Indians has put things into perspective,' Silas elaborated. 'They're happy to live the way they always have. But the zomb-augs are amassing. Plus we have other enemies, and we need to progress if we're to beat them.'

This was the first time Silas had mentioned the undead in John's presence, as though the AugFree leader considered the millions of monsters as an inconvenience rather than a threat to civilisation. 'So what do you want me to do?' John asked after a moment.

'Nothing right now. I just wanted to know if you'd be willing to help.'

'I'll do whatever I can.'

'Excellent. Now, report to Ambrosia. It's scavenging day.'

John almost stood to attention and saluted, but he suspected the joke would be lost on Silas. Instead he left and headed to Amber's room. Upon arrival he knocked on the door.

Amber answered quickly. She was dressed in overalls, though her hair was wrapped in a towel. 'Scavenging day, huh?' she said. 'Oh, could you do me a favour while I finish getting ready?'

'Sure.'

'I meant to give this to Silas when I met him first thing.' She handed him a notepad. 'Nothing interesting, just my log of events while he was away. Thanks.'

Within a minute, John was outside the chief's suite. He was about to press the doorbell when he heard a low voice. Presuming another member of the crew was with Silas, he decided to wait a minute before entering.

Curiosity overcame caution.

Glancing right and left to ensure no one else was in the corridor, he leaned against the door so that his ear nuzzled the uPVC.

'Well, what do you think?' Silas said.

There was a pause of approximately ten seconds. Then Silas spoke again. 'No. No one suspects anything.'

Another silence. The AugFree leader was obviously talking on a mobile communication device of some sort.

'Well, I might be able to do better than that. Picture this, instead of ten guys, ten robot killers.'

Silas was quiet again.

Then he laughed. 'Yeah, you heard right. And I have it on good authority, these things are lethal. One of them took out twenty bikers on its own.'

John wiped sweat from his brow and again checked over each shoulder.

'Who cares? They'll be surplus to requirements.'

Another break, this one just a couple of heartbeats.

'Friends? Friends are a luxury. Anyway, I'll call you later.'

The sound of footsteps set John's bowels twitching, but they were moving deeper into Silas's quarters, not in the direction of the door. Mind racing, he took a deep breath, counted to ten, rang the bell.

'Hold on!' Silas called. When he answered, his eyes narrowed for a moment, but he said nothing other than a 'thank you' for the diary.

***

'Everything okay?' Cait asked.

'Sure,' John lied. He'd been withdrawn since they left the base. Amongst the group, it was easier to hide, but Cait had been watching him closely for the last twenty minutes. His mind was a maelstrom. Of course, he'd known Silas was lying to him and keeping the others in the dark. But John hadn't thought the chief was planning to betray the gang he'd led for so long. He either had to warn them, or stand up to Silas himself.

'Watch your step,' Cait said. 'You need to be focussed out here.'

'Yeah, I know.' He worried, deep down, that he would do and say nothing. For he was a coward.

'Stop!' Amber called up ahead.

The group, now armed with the dead bikers' guns, halted. They were on a salvage mission, in a town about ten kilometres from Yonkers. Since arriving at the tower block, John had wondered how the AugFrees survived. Their food was provided by the allotments, pig pens and two cows, Daisy and Maisy. Their water was collected by a multitude of butts and cleansed with chemical powders. Heating and hot water was fuelled by solar power. However, some things, mundane items such as clothes, women's sanitary towels, toilet paper and the like, had to be sourced elsewhere. So today, the team were searching a warehouse that had once belonged to a convenience store chain. Partially gutted by fire and flood, it was a gloomy, damp place. It smelled of rotting vegetables and spoiled meat.

'Okay,' said Amber. 'Looks clear. Let's get what we can quickly and go.'

Upon arrival, Vincente, a dark, handsome man about thirty years old, had advised caution. Once a hunting enthusiast, the Puerto Rican native had a knack of spotting signs of recent zomb-aug activity. So far, though, his fears were yet to be justified. They moved into the building's main cargo store. The group remained in tight formation so that every person was in earshot. In pairs they began searching for the articles needed.

John was with Curls. He'd barely spoken to the youngster thus far, a situation he aimed to remedy. He reckoned that T and Cait would believe his account of Silas's clandestine chat. Conversely, Gideon and Cyril wouldn't even speak to him; they would doubtless alert their leader if they suspected John had a plan. It was the others, like Curls, he needed to work on. 'So,' he began, his tone casual. 'How long have you been with Amber and the others?'

'About six months.' Curls was scrabbling in a box. 'I'm the newest.'

'Except me.'

'Yeah. It's good, actually, not to be the noob.'

'Bet you're glad you found them.'

'Shit yeah. Probably be dead now, otherwise.'

You'll probably be dead soon anyway, John reflected privately. 'I'm just glad to not be alone,' he said.

'I hear that. I was —'

'Quiet!' hissed Vincente, who was paired with Amber.

Everybody dropped to a crouch, using the cardboard boxes as cover, then froze.

Apart from the dripping of water through the roof, there was silence.

And then came the noise they dreaded: the gasp of a zombie.

Chapter 19

'Anyone see it?' Amber asked.

No one answered.

Another verbalisation, this time from the opposite end of the storeroom.

'More than one,' whispered Curls.

'We're well-armed, though,' John said. 'Why can't we just shoot our way out?'

'The noise will attract others. That's one of the reasons we usually use crossbows and slings. Much quieter.'

'So why not bring them instead?'

'Dunno. Silas said we should take advantage. Not every day we get a load of guns dropped on our doorstep.'

'Quiet!' Gideon spat.

A moan from the direction of the first enemy. This time it was a female. Three zombs, now.

'Hold your fire,' Amber ordered. 'They might pass us by.'

This was a set-up. Silas had sent his crew with conventional weapons, knowing they would be loath to use them. Had John been more forthcoming with his suspicions, they could've taken precautions. Now it was his duty to get them out of this predicament.

He heard uneven footfalls getting closer. Steeling himself, he inched upwards to take a look over the crate behind which he was hidden. Just ten metres away was a zomb-aug. Slack-jawed and ponderous, it lurched one way then the other. Its chin was high, as if it was sniffing the air. It stopped; John quailed. It began walking once more. The thing's flesh had the grey hue to which John had become accustomed. Its shop clerk uniform was stained with old blood.

'Get down!' Curls said.

John obeyed, secretly thankful his heroic intentions had been foiled before they bore fruit. He drew his pistol, an ancient piece pilfered from a dead, hairy motorcyclist. He thumbed the safety switch.

A door's creak sounded.

The footsteps stopped.

Curls held her machine pistol two-handed and bounced on her haunches.

The zomb closest to them growled.

Another, this one to John's rear, answered in the same manner.

'Fuck this!' shouted Tyler. His gangling frame appeared above a box. He levelled his shotgun and fired in one motion.

Instinctively John ducked.

A snarl and a thud followed the gun's bang; Curls and John winced. Then there was a split-second of silence.

'Open fire!' Amber roared. 'Shoot your way clear!'

Curls stood and fired two bursts.

Grimacing at the din, John cowered for a moment. But the sight of a kid half his age reacting without hesitation shamed him into action.

He rose to a stoop and pointed his gun towards the closest exit.

'Come on, John.' Curls skipped past him.

There had been three zomb-augs in the storeroom. Now there were more. Ragged gunfire was deafening in the confined space - the tinkle of shattering glass against the staccato of rapid-fire rounds.

John saw one of the monsters bobbing and staggering; he aimed his handgun and fired. His bullets flew wide, but Curls's eye was more practiced.

'Stick with me,' she told him, beckoning. 'Don't fire till you're close, they can't shoot back, remember.'

'Got one!' Juarez said somewhere to their right.

'Ah, shit,' T cursed from their left. 'There's a whole mess of them coming from the south exit.'

'Right,' Curls said. 'East it is.'

With its box-sided corridors, the warehouse interior was like a maze. Although its floor area was just a couple of hectares, the layout made it feel both vast and crowded at the same time. At points, the containers were piled two metres high, so visibility was limited. And then, they would pass a gap, where the storage was stacked low, and a zombie's face would appear.

'Shit!' John said at one such juncture. Without hesitation he sighted the squat zomb and pulled the trigger. He was rewarded by the splatter of brains against cardboard.

'Good work,' said Curls whilst killing one on her side. 'Come on, I recognise this bit. We're close to the way we came in.'

A blood-curdling scream had them exchanging glances. One of their number was no more.

At the next intersection, they shared a heart-stopping moment with Tyler and Amber. Both rounding corners simultaneously, they almost mistook each other for hostiles.

'Jesus,' Tyler leaned against a crate, his wiry frame shaking. 'We almost clear?'

They were his last coherent words. The box taking his weight was snatched away. His arm was seized. He was dragged into the parallel corridor.

John and Curls grabbed his ankles, but the predator was too strong. Tyler's screech was cut short. Wet, sludgy thumps were followed by a tearing sound. Blood splatter appeared on the floor.

Amber shot one zomb, then another. But by the time the threat was eliminated, it was too late. When they hauled Tyler back through the gap, he was obviously dead. His eyes had been gouged with such force that the upper half of his face had crumpled, and his throat was gaping wide and red.

Fighting his stomach's rebellion, John turned away.

'No time for that.' Amber reloaded her gun. 'Let's go.'

Between them the AugFrees battled their way out of the storage depot. Two bikes were left behind. One was Tyler's. The other belonged to Chan, the young man who was a year or so older than Curls. John had hardly spoken to either, and for that he felt guilty.

***

When they arrived at HQ, John dismounted first. He strode ahead of the group, planning to prevent them from re-entering the tower block before he'd had a chance to make his point. He'd been rehearsing his words the whole way home.

Bemused by his manoeuvre, the others stopped.

'What's up, John?' Amber asked. She glanced at the windows of the building.

'We need to talk.' John aimed for a conciliatory tone, but his voice sounded timid.

'No we don't,' Gideon barked. 'We lost men, shit happens. Get out of the way.' He and his younger brother pushed past and entered the building.

'Okay, they don't want to listen,' said John. 'But the rest of you should.'

Eight pairs of eyes were fixed on the newest member of the crew. They were weary eyes, full of hurt. Juarez and T had injuries, not critical ones, but sufficiently serious to warrant medical attention. Certainly bad enough to sour their moods. Others had torn clothing, cuts, bruises. Although they'd slaughtered dozens of undead, they'd lost two of their own. One emotion not evident was patience. Even Cait and T were stony-faced.

'Spit it out, then.' Juarez was just over 160cm in height, but he was built like a bull, with a temper to match.

Momentarily John was lost for words. A brisk wind whipped his face; he felt isolated.

'We'll talk later, John,' Amber said.

'No, we need to talk now.' And John did talk. At length. He spoke without taking a breath for the first thirty seconds, and then for another couple of minutes. Once he was finished, the only sound was that of the wind. Studying their demeanours, he let out a long breath. He'd said all he could. They would either support him and overthrow the tyrant, or denounce him as a traitor and let Silas do as he saw fit.

Or there was the third option. One John hadn't even considered when he was rehearsing his entreaty on the way back from the salvage disaster. The depleted group's reticence was almost as chastening as the worst-case scenario. Amber,

T and Cait were the only AugFrees to meet his gaze as they passed.

The mixture of pity and fear in their expressions chilled John to the core.

***

Later on, after hours of solitude, John was in bed when there was rap on his door. It was the sound he'd been dreading all evening. The gentle thud was a gong's clash; his empty stomach recoiled.

However, upon answering, he was surprised, for his visitor wasn't Silas, Cyril or Gideon. There stood Amber, dressed in casual clothing, her hair tied back. She said nothing at first; for a brief, sickening moment John's relief turned to dismay. She'd come to summon him to await her master's judgment. Then she smiled, curtly but sweetly. He let her in and shut the door behind her, gripping the handle tightly to hide the tremble in his hands.

'I'm just going to start talking like you did before and I don't want you interrupt me or say anything until I'm completely finished because I've got to say it all.' She took a breath. 'Okay?'

'Of course. Why don't we sit down?'

They sat at opposite ends of a three seater settee.

'It's not easy for us here, John. This... this situation has been brewing for a while, and now that it's finally come to a head, I feel sorta glad and terrified at the same time. You see, Silas has looked after us for a long time. He used to be so protective, so on our side. It's only recently he's been acting weird.

'I mean, he's always been kinda weird, but more in a "I'll kill anyone who bothers you," scary big brother kinda way. Now though, something's changed. He's changed. But that doesn't mean that everyone else is gonna change too. Some people just wanna hide their heads in the sand and pretend he has some kind of plan up his sleeve. They can't accept that maybe he just doesn't give a shit nowadays.'

John waited, expecting the monologue to continue.

But Amber had clammed up. Now she folded her arms and bit her lip.

'Okay.' He selected his words with care. 'So are you referring to everyone else, or are you including yourself in this assessment?'

'Me more than anyone, I guess.' There was the slightest slur in her voice; perhaps she'd indulged in some of Cait's narcs. 'But then not at all. I know that sounds odd. I suppose my head wants me to break free but my heart is still… stuck.'

'Is there something… going on between you?'

'No.' She blushed charmingly. 'It's not like that. I don't even think Silas is interested in women, and he's really not my type.'

'Help me out, then. What is it that stops you doing what should be done?'

'It's not something I like to talk about.'

'Fair enough.' He smiled. 'I'm going to have a drink. Want one? I only got hot drinks, trying to cut out the —'

She stopped him with a single raised hand. Then she told her story. Amber was raised by her father, who was a well-meaning yet weak man. One of his schoolmates, an equally-bland civil servant, was a paedophile. Although he never raped adolescent Amber, he attempted to do so on two occasions. Both times the young girl fought back. After the first attack, she told her dad, who said he'd deal with the matter. Somehow, the pervert persuaded his friend that the incident was a misunderstanding. They were no longer on good terms, but the authorities were not informed. One night, on the way home from a friend's house, Amber was attacked again. Sure enough, the guilty party was the man she'd accused a few weeks earlier. Furious with her father, fifteen year-old Amber ran away from home.

She spent three years on and off the streets. Drug addictions almost claimed her life; New York City was as harsh as ever for the homeless. For a while she was part of a community of anti-capitalists. They were relatively happy years, until one of the group's seniors took a liking to the pretty young woman. Again she was forced to run. And she ran straight into the organisation which would eventually become NYC's AugFrees.

Their charismatic chief seemed so different to the predatory males that'd sullied her youth. Uninterested in her sexually, Silas sheltered and succoured Amber, while teaching her to embrace her own wildness. He harnessed her bravery, her rebellious streak, her refusal to surrender to those who would victimise her.

'He saved me.' Her eyes were moist. 'He was a good man.'

'"*Was*," though, Amber. That's the problem.'

'I know. I know. I just don't think I can go against him after everything he's done for me.'

'Even if you know he's a danger to you, to everyone else? He's probably responsible for the deaths of Tyler and Chan. And he did it deliberately.'

Now the tears were streaming from her eyes.

Gently John stemmed their flows with a forefinger. 'Come on. Crying doesn't suit you.'

She leaned across and kissed him softly on the lips.

It was the most fleeting of gestures, but it stirred within John a heat he'd long forgotten. Sensing Amber's fragility, he didn't push for more.

She stared into his eyes, her expression unreadable. Then she excused herself and left John alone.

He went to bed. The conversation and the kiss competed in his headspace for a time, until he resolved to impose order on his thoughts. Although Silas was intimidating, he had no hold over John. The man's threat wasn't suffused with a misplaced loyalty as it was with the others.

The solution was clear: Silas had to be removed before he caused more deaths, before he achieved his crackpot goals. And there was only one person capable of challenging him. Only one of the AugFrees wasn't enthralled by their leader. If he could overcome his natural timidity, John could make a difference, save lives. Like a real hero. But first, he would have to face a killer.

***

Snakes, panthers and zombies plagued John's dreams. Not zomb-augs, though – they were traditional brain-hungry ghouls, risen from the grave. When he woke he did so as if injected with adrenaline. He sat bolt upright, climbed out of bed and dressed himself. Treading silently, he crossed the room to look out of the window. Dawn was breaking. It would be a long day, he knew, an arduous battle against the odds. Because today he was going to confront Silas, man-to-man. Hand-to-hand if necessary. He'd never subscribed to any form of spirituality, but he believed it was his destiny to face Silas.

'Destiny,' he muttered to himself. He chuckled, quietly at first, then a little louder. 'Destiny!'

What an idiot.

No amount of self-ridicule or rationalisation could change his mind, however. John told himself he was a fool, risking his life to impress a female. In truth, though, that wasn't the reason. He wanted to do the right thing. He wanted —

'Jonathan?' The voice came from the doorway; it was followed by a knock. 'John?'

Shit. It was Silas.

Chapter 20

Suddenly John's palms were damp. His mouth was dry. Puffing out his chest and rolling his shoulders, he answered the door. 'Silas? It's early.'

'It is.' The big man looked sheepish. 'I thought you had someone in there with you. Heard you laughing.'

'No, it's just me.'

'Good. I want you to come with me. You and I are going on a little road trip.'

John breathed in through his nostrils. Taut and fuelled by hormones, he was tempted to tell Silas to go to hell. Instead, discretion prevailed. 'Sure, where to?'

***

Though glad they were travelling by motorcycle rather than horse, John had questions. What was Silas planning? Clearly, he saw the rest of the AugFrees as extraneous. John was useful because of his ability to build, train and operate droids and unmanned aerial vehicles. But if he were of value, why was he sent on a salvage mission that was doomed to failure? Perhaps he'd been paranoid, seeing connivance where there had been none. Perhaps Silas hadn't considered that firearms would make the team less safe. Perhaps John had misheard the telephone conversation Silas had shared.

It was a sunny morning, with occasional showers. The treacherous combination of low sunlight and puddled roads meant the two travellers rode slowly. There were no signs of life – human or undead – on the road.

Attached to the rear of Silas's bike was a trailer for transporting the printer, so the trip home would take even longer. Of course, there wouldn't be a return journey for one of them. Not if John found the courage to confront Silas. However, the closer they got to Asquith's, the stronger the former's doubts became. If the AugFree leader did confess to his newest recruit's accusations, was John brave enough to act? Moreover, did he stand a chance against a larger, more experienced fighter like Silas?

John's fears were interrupted by arrival at their destination. For a moment John stood and stared at Asquith's; memories of loneliness, fear and desperation distracted him from the obvious. Suddenly he realised: 'I thought you said the place is a wreck?' He studied Silas's face. 'You said it was almost burnt to the ground.'

'I know I did, John.' The bigger man climbed off his bike. 'I'm sorry. I can explain, and I will. But let's get inside first. Those clouds are heading this way.'

John looked at the iron sky to the east. Still watching Silas, he dismounted and lifted the hatch covering the key code pad next to the east wall's entry. 'After you,' he said as the doors swung open. He drew his pistol.

'I don't think that'll be necessary.' Silas left his own gun holstered.

Once they were indoors, John directed Silas towards the workshop, letting him lead the way. 'So,' he began. 'Are you going to explain why you lied?'

'That was for our benefit.'

'*Our* benefit? Mine and yours?'

'Yes, John.' Silas's tone was friendly. 'Yours and mine. I didn't want the others to know about our plans.'

'We don't have any plans, Silas.'

'Oh, but we do. You and I are going to create a little army together. An army of robots capable of great things.'

'And the others?' John indicated the workshop's entrance. 'Where do they fit into all this?'

'They don't.' Silas pushed open the door. 'We don't need them. We only need me, because I'm the leader, and you, because you're the engineer.'

John put a hand to his hip. The gun's cool metal comforted him, as did the familiar smell of the workshop.

'I know you heard the telephone conversation I had. I also know that Amber deliberately sent you with that diary because she thought you'd catch me on the phone. I took a gamble by sending you to an area that I knew was infested by zomb-augs, but I knew that if you survived, you'd try and convince the rest that I was going to cut them loose.' He pointed at the printer. 'Is that the printer?'

'Yeah, that's it. But why? What did you have to gain from me exposing you?'

'Because it would prove to you how weak they are, how useless they are, when they chose not to believe you.'

John shook his head. 'Just because they've allowed you to head-fuck them, doesn't mean they're weak. They're good people.'

'That they may be, but they *are* weak. And there's no place in this world for the weak.'

'Was it worth the risk, though? The risk that they'd follow me, just to prove a point?'

'That wasn't a risk, John. Because you're not a leader. They are followers, but they will only follow a leader. And that's not you.'

There was a glint in the other man's eyes which reminded John of the Pro-Church fanatics he used to see ranting on street corners. Silas's calmness and self-possession were a well-practised veneer; lunacy bubbled beneath the surface. Most frightening was his tendency to refer to human beings as commodities, his to utilise or jettison when appropriate. How had the other AugFrees not seen the truth? He was their saviour at one point, but not any longer. When did he become this monster standing before John?

'You're wondering, aren't you?' The corners of Silas's mouth twitched; he was suppressing a grin.

John's right hand crept towards the pistol at his belt. He said nothing.

'You're wondering how I tricked them all into thinking I'm a great guy.'

Eyes narrowed, John gave the slightest of nods.

'Truth is, I *was* a great guy. That's why they love me. But I got sick of being a great guy. Sick of changing diapers, sick of putting band-aids on cut knees. Sick of sacrificing my own future for those clowns.'

'The others aren't to blame, though. They say it's *you* who's reactionary, who's scared of progress. *You're* the one terrified of tech.'

'Yeah, well. I've changed my mind about that. Guy's got a right to change his mind, don't he? Besides, I've made an alliance, but with the bikers, not the Comanches.'

'What about the main group of AugFrees?'

'I'm not interested in them. They offered to let us join them, but I didn't like their terms.'

'You mean you wouldn't be a chief anymore. You'd have to submit to someone else.'

'I guess.' Silas sighed. 'I've disappointed you, haven't I? Well if that's the case, *you*'ve disappointed me. I thought you'd be forward-thinking, flexible. You defended yourself, then you branched out, you had the guts to make a move on me. But it turns out you're just as gutless as they are.' He looked at his mucky boots, then back at John. 'Shame.'

'Who says I'm disappointed? Like you said, we could achieve great things together with the right tools.' John pointed at the 3D printer. 'And that, to me, looks like the right tool. Want to take a look?'

Silas nodded. 'Excellent.' As he turned and approached the machine, John drew his gun.

'This is a thing of beauty.' The AugFree leader was enraptured by the printer. He tinkered, prodded, examined. 'In a way, it's this kind of contraption which sums up the whole zomb-augpocalypse, shit-hitting-the-fan scenario. We got too sure of ourselves, us humans. Too arrogant. Thought if we *could* create something, then we *should* create it. And to hell with the consequences.'

Licking dry lips, John raised his gun.

Chapter 21

'Sold our souls to the Devil, and he leased them back. But we defaulted on the repayments.' Silas sniggered. Abruptly he spun on his heel. When he saw the barrel pointing at his head, he raised his hands theatrically. 'Oh no, please!' he lisped. 'Don't shoot!'

'I don't have to.' John was surprised by the firmness of his own voice. 'But it ends here, Silas. You leave the tower, leave the whole damned state, and never come back.'

'Well I suppose I'd better do as you say, then. One problem, John, that gun. Who gave it you this morning before we set out?'

'You did.' John's bowels fluttered.

'Did you check it was loaded?'

They stood five metres apart. Silas was poised, the stillness of his bulk as threatening as the advance that was sure to follow.

Dumbly, John turned the gun to look at its barrel. As if that would confirm or deny Silas's claim.

The smile disappeared from the big man's meaty jaws. It was replaced by a blank expression. Silas pounced. Deceptively quick, he was upon John in an instant. He batted away puny arms and landed a sickening blow to the smaller man's sternum.

John was dying. He must've been, because his lungs had stopped working. Breathing wasn't difficult; it was impossible. Wheezing piteously, he sank to his knees. Drool pooled on the concrete floor as he gaped like a prize trout. The pain was overwhelming.

'There are three ways we can do this, Jonathan.' Silas spoke as if discussing the weather. 'One, you do what I say, when I say, and you get a quick death. As will Amber and the rest, and you have my word on that. Two, you fool me around, I beat your ass, you do what I say anyway, then I kill you all painfully.' Silas's right paw cupped John's jaw. He tilted John's head back to look him in the eye. 'Three, somehow, you don't surrender to the beating, and I kill you by accident.'

Mastering an urge to vomit, John struggled to rise to his feet. He wasn't a proud man. But whatever happened, he wouldn't die on his knees. 'Okay,' he gasped. 'I'll help. Just don't hurt the others. This is on me. I'm the one who turned on you, not them.'

'Right. I'll re-evaluate when you've finished your work. Do a good job and I might even settle for crippling you.'

According to Silas, by completing the job, John would leave behind a legacy. For that he should've been grateful. Using his skills, he was to create a replica of Frank that was loyal only to Silas. The new bot would have one advantage, however: the skill to build others like itself. It would be programmed with the ability to program the 3D printer, making its architect obsolete.

A simple enough idea, John admitted. In theory. The most he could promise was that he would do his utmost to deliver.

His "best shot" wouldn't save Amber and her friends from the bikers when Silas sneaked them into the tower block, though. 'Just get it done, no excuses,' the AugFree leader growled. 'Or the last thing you'll see will be footage of your buddies being executed. Slowly.' Only now did Silas draw his own pistol. He collected John's from the floor and ejected the magazine, held it aloft, and then clicked it back into place. 'Looks like it was loaded after all,' he said with a smirk.

For the first time since he'd been hit, John felt something other than agony and despair. He'd been duped. By having the nerve to attack with his fists rather than going for his gun, Silas had convinced John that his weapon was useless.

'Come on, get to work.' Silas's grin was widening in response to John's ire. 'Don't be sore, I've tricked smarter guys than you.'

Pretending resignation, John switched on the computer and the printer. He loaded the latter with scrap and set it to run on the formula that was used for Frank. 'I'll need some other equipment.'

'Get what you need. But no games. The first robot you build better be subservient to me only, or there'll be trouble.' Silas chambered a round in his handgun. 'Lead the way, we'll go and fetch what you need together.'

As they headed to the south tower, John's mind buzzed. Ridiculously, Silas's "tricked smarter guys than you" remark stung more than anything else. He retrieved the item he needed, stating that it was an integral component in the build process. Although he looked dubious, Silas seemed to accept his explanation.

Back in the workshop, John checked the printer's progress. Then he sat at his computer terminal and cracked his knuckles. He synced the device he'd got from the south tower with the computer's operating system. Contemplating the difficulty of the task at hand, he clicked his tongue. After he'd made a virtual copy of Frank's bespoke programme, he began to make alterations to the script. His hands were clammy. If his captor realised he was being tricked – which, given his paranoia, was a very real possibility – the consequences would be dire.

Silas watched at first. Flummoxed by the technological wizardry, he soon grew bored and stopped paying attention.

Instead of adding to Frank's recipe, John subtracted. The resulting cyborg would be compliant but dull-minded. Capable of following basic instructions: walk forwards, turn around, shoot that target, et cetera. Moreover, it would self-destroy before it could harm anyone at Yonkers.

Before long the amendments were finished. John didn't tell Silas, though. Instead, he secretly began the second, more taxing step of his plan. He wasn't even sure it would be successful. He was risking a painful death and retribution against Amber and the others into the bargain. But John suspected that even if he did satisfy Silas's request, his new friends' lives were forfeit. He had nothing to lose.

'What now?' Silas asked when his captive stood.

'We wait.' John grimaced in apology. 'The program assimilation is fast, but this is an old printer.'

'Whatever. Just do it as quickly as possible.'

'Well, if we compromise on aesthetics, we can be done in two hours.'

'What does compromising on aesthetics entail?'

'The bot will be humanoid, bipedal, but it'll look… basic. Like a kid's sketch.'

'Fuck it, that'll be dandy.'

***

One hundred and twenty-four minutes later, John's newest progeny was born. The two humans stood side-by-side in the workshop, watching the cyborg as it came to life. Unbeknownst to its adopted father, its maximum lifespan was four hours. By then, though, either John or Silas would be dead.

The latter tried to hide his excitement; the numerous successive questions he asked belied his stoicism.

'First things first,' John's tone was as firm as he dared. 'We need to test its basic command-following faculties.'

'But you've programmed it yourself.' Silas scowled. 'You know what it's capable of.'

'Yeah, you'd think so. But that's the mistake I made with the first bot I built. I didn't test it, moved straight to advanced stuff, nearly cost me my life.'

Silas turned and glowered. His fists were bunched.

Inwardly cringing, John affected insouciance. 'It's your call, Silas. But if things go south, and I'm killed, will you be able to fix it? Frank's older brother had a glitch that turned him into a psycho. Just a really simple error, too.'

'Fine. Let's go outside, then. Is everything still set up from when you tested Frank?'

John confirmed that it was. As they left the workshop, he grabbed the control he'd taken from the watchtower.

***

Silas nodded in begrudged approval. 'Looks like you were real thorough, John. Shame things didn't work out between us, we could've been a force to be reckoned with.' He looked at Frank Jr. 'Is he ready?'

'Yeah,' John croaked. He cleared his throat. 'He's ready. You command him, I'll keep an eye on his readouts on here, ready to shut down if necessary.' He nodded at the device in his hands. Please, he prayed, licking sweat from his upper lip, don't ask to look at the remote.

But Silas was too engrossed by his synthetic protégé. He directed Junior around the obstacle course, cheering when targets were reduced to smithereens. Then master and apprentice had a shooting contest, which was dominated by the machine. In the meantime, John fiddled with the controller. Although he glanced occasionally at the competing pair, he became absorbed with his efforts. He barely noticed when the gunfire died away.

'You're real interested in that "reader" of yours, John.' Silas baritone sent chills down John's spine. 'Let me see.'

'Just hang on,' John stammered.

'Why? What are you doing?' Silas began to approach.

'N-n-nothing.' John backed away, still intent on the tablet in his hands. Just a few more seconds…

'Let. Me. See.' Silas reached out to seize the object in question. Then a noise overhead caught his attention: the hum of a drone.

Using the distraction to his advantage, John pulled away. He didn't look up because he didn't need to. Instead he tapped the screen twice, once to target Silas, once to open fire.

Realising the danger, Silas threw himself at John, knocking the remote control from his hand.

Ten metres above the UAV's cannon roared.

John scrabbled away, desperate to reach the remote, but Silas's bellow stopped him short. The big man was on his back, and he was hurt, grievously. Blood gushed from a hole in his gut. His left hand was soaked in crimson as he failed to stem the flow. His right still held his gun. 'Fuck you,' he said, aiming unsteadily at the man who'd killed him.

John ducked; the pistol fired.

Agony erupted in John's left arm. He screamed and fell to the floor. Craning his neck, he saw Silas point the weapon. The muzzle was dark and wide. A series of memories flashed past John's mind's eye. The trigger clicked. But no bang. Click, click, click. No bang. Silas groaned and then fell silent.

The liquid burn of the bullet wound began to lessen. Suddenly John was exhausted. His eyelids were drooping, his limbs like lead. The sun above was bright, but it was getting dimmer by the second.

Chapter 22

Every time John thought he'd woken, he was soon terrified by the reality. He hadn't woken after all. He was either in a coma, or he was dead. But each time, for a few muzzy seconds, minutes or hours, he was jubilant. Gifted a second shot at life, and free from injury, he went about his business. Until he realised that this new life wasn't "normal," not even by his recent standards. Trips to the tops of mountains, conversations with well-spoken animals, flights from dinosaurs – events which proved he was still unconscious. Whether or not he was permanently asleep, he couldn't say. He stopped caring after a while.

The latest chapter of his comatose/dead existence began in much the same way as any of its predecessors. He woke slowly. His eyes were gummed, his mouth arid. His arm was connected to an intravenous drip, which wasn't uncommon in these dreams. But this time, when he tried to remove the needle, he felt a sting. Plus, he felt exhausted; the desire to drift back to sleep was overwhelming.

He was awake.

He was in the same room in which he'd recovered from the motorcycle crash. This time he was in more pain, with his arm the chief culprit. His right sleeve had been cut away. On his bare arm, there was a white dressing, in the middle of which was a circle of red. Silas had shot him.

And Silas had died. Hadn't he?

How had John made his way back to the tower, though?

What had happened to everyone else?

The questions competed against the fog in his mind: a need for clarity versus a compulsion to rest. 'Hello?' he called. His tongue was too large for his mouth, and his voice sounded unfamiliar. 'Anybody? Hello!'

The door opened. John cowered for a moment; then he saw Frank.

'Hello, John,' Frank said. 'How do you feel?'

'Like shit. Am I really awake?'

'Yes. For the first time in three days. If I were capable of worrying, I would've been worried.'

'But you were... I was... What happened?'

'You killed Silas. He shot you. You were shot, so one of my override protocols was triggered. I was resuscitated, and I came and got you.'

'Protocols? I didn't even know you had "protocols." How did you know where I was?'

'I always know where you are. When I'm active.'

'No shit?' John shook his head in wonder; the movement hurt.

'No shit.' Frank smiled. 'You're safe now, but you need to rest.'

Inexplicably, John felt tears in his eyes.

Frank pretended not to notice.

***

John's recovery was swift. Exsanguination aside, he wasn't badly injured. The bullet had caused muscle damage, which would heal in time, after a few weeks of pain. Tendons, ligaments, bones and nerves were unscathed; John was a lucky boy, according to Frank. The cyborg was programmed with field hospital skills, and he was the closest thing to a doctor.

Cait and T visited frequently. They apologised for not supporting John after the disaster in the warehouse, but he told them they were forgiven. Spending hours at a time with the patient, Amber was most attentive. All three accepted without question his account of events at Asquith's, though some of the others weren't as receptive. Unsurprisingly, Gideon and Cyril stayed away. They were angry with John, apparently. They believed he'd double-crossed Silas.

***

'So what now?' John winced as he donned a jacket. He waved away Amber's offer to assist.

'What now?' she echoed. 'I don't know. You still need to take it easy, it's only a week since you were almost killed. Let's just take it slowly.'

'I know, I know.' John unlocked the front door and held it open for Amber. 'But Silas had plans. He'd made contact with other people apart from the bikers. What's to stop us following up on that contact?'

'Slow down!' Amber said, hurrying to catch up. 'A little light exercise, Frank said. A nice walk through the neighbourhood. Not a quick-march. Anyway, whoever Silas was involved with is probably not the sort of person *we* want to be dealing with.'

'The bikers, obviously not. But the AugFrees he turned down? Shouldn't we at least search his room? See what we can find?'

'Okay. But first, fresh air. A little light exercise.'

***

Gideon and Cyril were like two faithful dogs. Unable to reconcile with the reality of their idol's demise and his betrayal, they jealously guarded his quarters. The former said, 'It's one thing we have to suffer his murderer walking around here as if he's done nothing wrong.' He glared at John. 'But to have him snooping around in Silas's room…'

'Well,' Amber said, 'if you truly care about his memory, you won't stand in my way. He chose *me* as his deputy, remember. You should respect that.'

'If he'd known you were gonna turn on him,' Cyril contended, 'he wouldn't have chosen you!'

'Somebody's got to be in charge,' said John. 'Otherwise nothing will get done. What about if we have a vote? Will you respect that?'

The two brothers, whose faces were identical shades of beetroot, considered the idea. After a minute they acquiesced.

So Amber called a meeting. Not for the first time, John reflected on the group's proclivity for suffrage, for debate. They lived in lawless times, their world a science fiction writer's fantasy, yet still they clung to philosophies from a bygone era. The AugFrees gathered in the dining room. Although the atmosphere was frosty, there was no open aggression. Barely a word was spoken as Amber distributed ballot papers. In true egalitarian spirit, every member was nominated.

Gideon and Cyril voted for each other. Everyone else but Amber named her; she opted for John.

'I hope we can move forwards now,' the newly-elected leader said.

Her detractors were sulky, but they nodded their assent.

***

John was still too sore to participate in mundane but necessary activities like tending to livestock and chopping wood. Amber had never shirked physical labour before, so when she excused herself to accompany John to investigate Silas's suite, no one complained. 'What exactly are you hoping to find?' she asked once he'd picked the lock.

'I don't know,' John said. 'The phone he was talking on, maybe.'

'Hmm.' Amber switched on the light. 'I just don't get how his phone would work. Cell networks are dead, have been for ages.'

'I don't know, it doesn't make sense.' John appraised Silas's lounge. It was clean and tidy, meticulously so. There was a three-seater sofa, an armchair, bookcase, bureau and dining table. 'How did you access the Internet when you posted your videos?'

'Satellite Internet is still good.' She opened the desk drawer and took out a notepad. 'The solar panels work, and you can hack into their supply if you know what you're doing. That's how I kept this old thing,' she took an antiquated smartphone from her pocket, 'juiced. But it only holds charge for an hour or so, battery's nearly dead.'

'Let me see.' John indicated the notepad. Most of the pages were blank, but some were covered in numbers and names. 'So if you could secretly get online, what's to stop Silas from doing the same?'

'No, no way.' Amber moved on to the bookshelves. She pulled out books, one at a time, and riffled through the pages. 'He hated anything...'

'Anything techy?' John was rummaging between couch cushions, taking care to keep his injured arm out of harm's way. 'Have you forgotten the recent revelations? About how he wasn't actually that bothered about tech and was just stringing you all along?'

'I know, I'm just so used to saying it. So yeah, I suppose he could've been accessing the net to make calls.'

The search of the living room and kitchen yielded no results, so they moved into the bedroom. It was equally functional and impersonal. There were no photographs or knick-knacks. John and Amber were thorough, but it made no difference; their efforts proved fruitless. The bathroom was their last resort, and with this in mind, they were even more painstaking.

'Fuck,' Amber concluded. 'There's nothing here.'

'Perhaps his secret intelligence bunker was somewhere else in the tower,' John said. 'Another apartment, maybe. How many are there?'

'Oh, just a few hundred. If we go through all of them, one at a time, we should have the whole building searched by the end of the year.'

'Not if it's in the first one we check! Think positive, Ambrosia.'

She gave him a funny look, then laughed; he chuckled along.

'Come on, let's go. We'll have to rethink. Maybe speak to the others, see if they have any suggestions.' His arm was aching; he was overdue some painkillers.

On their way out, Amber caught her foot on a rug that'd been displaced during their hunt. She didn't fall, but she stepped heavily on the laminated flooring.

'Hang on a sec,' said John. 'Your step, then, it sounded… weird.'

'Weird how?' Amber asked.

'Like, hollow. Wait a minute.' John squatted and examined the faux-wooden floor. Then he went back to the kitchen and fetched a knife. On his knees, he used the blade to prize the laminate strips apart. They separated easily, as if the action had been undertaken before. 'Give me a hand, it's tricky with one arm.'

Together John and Amber uncovered a trapdoor. It had a circular hole, roughly two centimetres in diameter, in one corner. They both smiled.

'The apartment below, is it anybody's?' he asked.

'Ah… no.'

'If he wanted to use the apartment below, then why not just go in and out through the door?'

She shrugged. 'I suppose he probably didn't want people to see him using the room, and start asking questions.' She poked two fingers through the hole in the wood and lifted the hatch. With the light from the lantern hanging from Silas's ceiling, a ladder was visible. John quickly forgot the burn in his arm.

Chapter 23

Another meeting. They were beginning to irritate John, which came as a surprise given how desperate for human contact he'd been a couple of weeks ago. It wasn't the frequency of the discussions that was wearing – it was the ongoing theme. He, Amber, Cait and T were willing to embrace change, to explore avenues for progress. Gideon and Cyril were always the opposition and would argue night was day just to be awkward. The rest were more reserved. Their ambivalence was almost as infuriating as the brothers' obstinacy. As a result, few decisions were made. The focus would typically veer away from the subject in question. Time was wasted, old grievances revisited.

'Look,' said John. His bullet wound throbbed; his temper was frayed. 'Can we stop arguing about the whys and wherefores? This morning, we discovered the location of the main AugFree base. A safe haven. Somewhere we don't have to worry about zombs and bikers, somewhere we can meet thousands of other survivors. We could be on our way there, right now. Instead, we're arguing about whether it was right to search Silas's room a week after his death! The guy lied to you, tried to kill me, said he was going to kill you. All of you. But —'

'So *you* say,' Gideon sneered. 'How do we know *you're* not lying?'

'Oh, for fucksake! Tell you what, why don't we have a vote?'

'We shouldn't be forced to leave if we don't want to.' Cyril pouted as if impressed by his own input.

'Nobody's forcing you.' Even Amber was beginning to lose her cool. 'How about this, whoever wants to go, can go. Whoever wants to stay, can stay.'

'Split up the group?' said Curls tremulously.

'Seems to me the group is already split,' observed John.

The group fell silent. AugFree membership was the only constant they'd had for the last couple of years. For everyone apart from John, it was the last remnant of ante-apocalyptic life. Cyril and Gideon included, they were stricken by the prospect of disunity.

John swallowed. He was the agent of change, the dynamite in the foundations. Did he have the right to tear these people asunder with his ambition?

Eventually, Gideon spoke, 'Listen. We don't want to do anything rash, is all. But that don't mean we want out.'

'Good,' replied Amber. 'We don't want that either. But just remember this. Silas, whatever his endgame, was looking to leave. He knew it was time.'

The decision was made, the die cast. John was given another week to recover from his gunshot. Subsequently: departure from the tower block and a journey to Charleston, West Virginia. If the maps and scrawlings from Silas's basement were accurate, the eight survivors, plus John and Frank, would soon join with their AugFree brethren.

***

However heartfelt their misgivings, Cyril and Gideon chose not to quit the AugFrees. But any hope the disharmony would be dispelled was dashed, for another argument ensued before they'd even left the parking lot. The brothers thought they should travel by bicycle. No one else favoured a 900km, three day push bike ride across three states. Of course, the motorbikes were noisy, but any zomb-augs that heard them would be swiftly outrun. They had sufficient gasoline, too. Either way, John's injury would be aggravated. Still, the suffering would be shorter-lived if the crew used the Harleys left by the bikers.

Thankfully, democracy came to the rescue. Armed with as much weaponry as they could carry, the AugFrees set off at ten AM, using the ten motorcycles that were in the best condition. John's arm hurt, but not too much. Amber had found muscle-regenerative meds on a salvage excursion six months ago. She'd been saving them for a rainy day, she said. Although his bicep wasn't as good as new, it'd improved dramatically.

As one the NYC AugFrees started their engines. The noise was glorious. It spoke of power, freedom, a new beginning. Over the din, Juarez shouted, 'Look!' He pointed. 'Dead ahead!'

Where the access road for the tower block met the main thoroughfare, a host of zomb-augs was amassing. There were at least a hundred of the freaks. And they were moving with urgency.

'They can choke on our exhaust fumes.' Cait's eyes shone.

'Come on,' Amber ordered. 'Let's go before they block the road.'

The crew rode away from their home in a ragged line and accelerated past the bemused zombs. The stench was indescribable, a cloying decay that clung to the nostrils. Grasping hands were foiled as they jostled each other to compete for the elusive quarry. John's arm ached; he was gripping the handlebars too tightly.

A familiar face was visible above the rank and file. It was Tyler. His gaunt face and scrawny limbs suited zombification, somehow. None of the others seemed to notice their former comrade.

As they left the monsters in their wake, John considered the presence of the undead AugFree. This was no zombie plague. The zomb-augs didn't add to their number by infecting those they killed, and Tyler was not augmented. So why had he turned? Not for the first time, John considered the most imponderable of puzzles. What did the zomb-augs *want*? Or rather, whoever was controlling them, what did *they* want? Surely their only goal wasn't to destroy everything in their path.

***

Before long the escapees were riding on the I-78 highway. They cruised at 100kph, not wanting to expend too much petroleum. There was no rush, after all. If they'd deciphered Silas's maps and notes correctly, the AugFree base in WV was a permanent installation, well-established and fortified.

The riders travelled in convoy. Amber was at the front. T brought up the rear. On a dry road, with only the occasional abandoned car or truck to overtake, they made good time.

With 50km to go, clouds massed overhead, and twilight came early. It'd been a fine day, sunny with a brisk wind, but the air pressure was dropping. Frank forecast a storm. Possibly a hurricane. Just as the first fat raindrops began to fall, they saw a small town to the south. A single plume of smoke rose from one of the buildings. They discussed seeking shelter and bedding down for the night; their decision was made for them by a faraway peal of thunder.

Rolling into the township, blinking away rain and dust, the travellers were watchful. The houses and shops appeared deserted, their barred windows dark. When they reached the town centre they dismounted. Again the heavens rumbled, and the steady rainfall became a downpour. The group splashed through puddles as they ran for cover. The town hall, a splendid structure in comparison to its neighbouring properties, had a covered entrance. They huddled in the doorway and watched the deluge in silence.

'Good place to rest up.' Curls patted the double doors.

'Yeah,' Cyril replied. 'If we can get in.'

John was about to employ his house-breaking skills when T pushed one of the doors open.

'It's open,' Vincente remarked.

'No shit,' said Cait.

***

In the morning, John woke earlier than the others. He came to with a start; his dreams had been plagued by an undead Silas taking potshots at his head. A sunbeam shone through a gap in the planks nailed across one of the windows; its light fell on his face. He cast aside his blanket, grimacing at the pain in his arm, and yawned. On the floor around him, the others still slept. Some were snoring, others silent. Groaning with stiffness, John rose to his feet.

At the door stood Frank, a shotgun in one hand. He turned when his master's knees cracked.

'What time is it, Frank?'

'Nine minutes to six.' Frank turned back to face the window next to the door.

'Anything to report?' John tilted his head to ease the tension in his neck.

'Yes. The locals are stirring.'

'Zombs?'

'No. Humans. Three times I've seen them pass, and they're acting suspiciously.'

John stood side by side with his cyborg and peered through the glass. Apart from a cat and two birds, the street was deserted. 'We saw no one when we recced last night.'

'They probably heard the motorcycles and assumed the Hell's Angels were here, so they hid. When we didn't set fire to everything or loot, they realised we were somebody else. Now they're curious.'

'Or so you presume.'

'Yes,' Frank allowed, 'it is a supposition. But one with a 54% chance of being correct.'

One of the others was stirring: it was Cait. She'd admitted the previous evening that she was a light sleeper.

'Sorry,' John whispered.

'Don't worry about it.' She got up and joined John and Frank by the entrance. She rubbed her eyes and stared out of the window. 'Looks like an early start would be wise, anyway.'

'Yeah?' John. 'Why, what's wrong?'

Frank appeared equally confused. Although he'd spotted people in the vicinity, he obviously hadn't deemed them enough of a threat to warrant concern.

'See that smoke?' Cait said.

'Yeah.' John shrugged. 'Same smoke we saw from the interstate yesterday. We checked the building last night, remember, and it looked deserted. Probably just an old burnt-out fuel cell, Gideon said.'

'Same source, not the same smoke.'

'What do you mean? Smoke is smoke.'

'Look at it.'

'I've seen it, it's the same! What are you talking about?'

'She's right,' Frank interjected. 'It's not the same. It's not a steady stream.'

'Like smoke signals.' Cait folded her arms.

John looked again: the other two were right. 'What does it mean? Could it be the Comanches?'

Cait laughed. 'This isn't the Wild West, John. No, if it was the Comanches, they'd have ambushed us in the open. They wouldn't lay a siege.'

'Who then?'

'I don't know. You've not seen anyone?'

Without turning away from the window, Frank repeated the report given to John. He added that the persons he'd seen were mainly Caucasian, not Native.

The trio discussed the situation in hushed voices. Clearly, the townsfolk were spreading news of their unwitting visitors. But did that mean they were a threat? Were they plotting a violent eviction of the AugFrees? Or were they simply cautious of outsiders? The latter was a strong possibility, considering the dangers posed by biker gangs, indigenous tribes and zombies.

Eventually, the chatter roused their friends, so Cait apprised them of developments. Juarez, Gideon, Vincente, Curls and Cyril were convinced they'd walked into a trap. The rest were more relaxed. The worriers infuriated the optimists with their hysteria, and the optimists infuriated the worriers with their complacency. Soon, they were arguing.

Apart from Frank. After half an hour or so, he silenced them. 'Look. Be quiet, and look.'

Outside, a team of men were dragging a Christian cross across the green. At least four metres high, and two wide, it was painted white. Its stump was sharpened like a stake. The group was a mixture of races, ages and sizes, but not genders. Without once looking in the direction of the town hall, they heaved the symbol into place, using ropes tethered to its arms to pull it into the green. When they were finished, the individuals kneeled before the cross, heads bowed. There they remained for at least twenty minutes. Suddenly, they stood as one. The shortest was no older than sixteen. He marched away from his brethren. Then he returned with a large bucket. As the others continued to pray, the boy slung the contents of his pail over the cross, taking care to douse as much as possible of the ivory with scarlet.

'Is that blood?' Juarez asked.

'If it ain't, it's sure meant to be,' said T. 'Some Pro-Churchers worship the blood-soaked cross.'

Chapter 24

He didn't recognise the man's name.

'Shit, John,' Cait said. 'You honestly never watched *any* TH? He was huge.'

John had had a tele-holojector before the apocalypse, but he only used it for movies and documentaries. 'Honestly. His face looks familiar, I suppose. I thought he looks like a sportsman.'

'He was,' T chuckled. 'Sorta. More like a hunter.'

John was nonplussed.

'He used to travel the world, looking for girls to seduce.' Vincente's dark eyebrows beetled. 'It was a shitty show, truth be told.'

'And now he's the leader of a Pro-Church sect.' John shook his head. 'That's… bizarre.'

'Yeah, a pretty big sect, by the looks of it,' Amber said. She was still stood at the window with Frank. 'There must be about a thousand of them out there, so let's stop reminiscing and work out a way out of this.'

'One thousand and seventy-six, to be exact,' Frank said. 'I'm working on a solution now.'

Cyril sneered. 'Oh, we'll be alright, then.'

John suggested that the men outside may not be hostile.

His hopes were dashed by Curls, who insisted that the only way to avoid violence was to submit to the Pro-Churchers' demands.

'Shouldn't we at least speak to them, though?' John said. 'We'll have no chance if we try to fight our way out.'

The others agreed. Using an old tablecloth and an unopened tin of paint, the AugFrees made a sign that said, "WE COME IN PEACE." They held it against the glass front door for five minutes. And they waited. Those knelt in prayer didn't respond; they had their backs to the building so couldn't see it. However, the celebrity, Kelvin Curcic, who'd been flitting in and out of view for the last hour or so, seemed to acknowledge their message. Alone, he swaggered their way. His smile was dazzling in the morning sun.

'What's the deal with his teeth?' John asked.

'They're encrusted with diamonds, apparently,' said Amber. 'Though they're probably synthetic.'

'And that makes him better at getting girls on this show of his?'

'*Made* him better. Doubt they're still producing it, somehow. Does nothing for me, anyway.'

Curcic was soon in the doorway. With a fist bedecked in gold rings, he rapped on the pane.

Frank eyed him dispassionately and then turned to Amber.

'Let him in,' she said.

At about 190cm in height, and a lean 100kg in weight, the preacher was an impressive figure. The overcoat he wore was plain but clean, expensive but understated. He had an easy charm. His voice was as rich as his coffee-coloured eyes. 'The best of the Lord's blessings, folks!' He made eye contact with each individual present and offered a tanned hand to Amber. 'I take it you're the boss?'

With a wry smile, she accepted the gesture. 'Pretty much.'

'Well, that's just dandy. Not how we do things, I'll grant you. We like to *take care* of our womenfolk. But we're nothing if not tolerant.'

Cait snorted. '"Tolerant"?'

Curcic's countenance darkened for an instant, but he promptly reactivated the megawatt grin. 'Yes, tolerant. That's why we're going to give you six hours.'

'Six hours to do what?' asked Gideon.

'To submit to the Lord God Almighty and join us.'

'And if we don't?' Amber said.

'Our tolerance becomes intolerance. I'm sure you've heard of what happens to those who defy the Lord and reject His mercy?'

Nobody spoke.

'We've got a bunch of clean, white crosses, just begging to be soaked in red. And we need fresh blood. Like I said, you've got six hours to choose. If you make me come back here, we'll crucify every last one of you.'

***

The United States of America was, for a considerable period, one of the most religious countries in the world. Until twenty-one years ago, at least, when one of the most devastating earthquakes in Italian history destroyed the town of Amatrice. Undiscovered Ancient Roman ruins were unearthed. They were authenticated by archaeologists and dated back to the second century BC. Scrolls were found which told the tale of Jesus Christ and his disciples – two hundred years before their supposed occurrence. Virtually every miracle depicted in the Bible had already been committed, but in a different locale. The fate of the "Messiah," Marcus, a former slave who convinced his owner to emancipate him, was identical to that of Jesus.

'I know all this,' said John when Vincente had finished speaking. 'But what difference does it make to us?'

One hour had passed; they had five left.

'Those that are still religious after everything the Amatrice scrolls revealed, are almost certainly insane,' Juarez said. 'No offence, T.'

T laughed. 'Those papers could've been planted —'

'Like dinosaur bones?' Cait snorted.

'Still, though, how does this help us?' John said the last five words slowly and deliberately.

'It's quite obvious, isn't it?' Frank said, startling the others. He'd been silent thus far.

'This should be good,' Cyril muttered. 'Our pet guard dog thinks he's a clever boy.'

Gideon smirked, but everyone else waited for Frank to continue.

'They're not the most intelligent people,' Frank continued. 'Well, perhaps that's the wrong way of putting it. They're more gullible than the average human.'

'They believe what they want to believe,' Curls said, almost to herself. 'I have an idea.'

***

Nine crosses cast nine cross shadows on the grass. Over a thousand acolytes, their dress almost Puritan in its simplicity, stood as still as the wooden structures before them. A few coughs and baby squalls aside, there was silence. The kneeling penitents, formerly known as AugFrees, waited with their hands clasped. Carrion birds wheeled and cawed above.

Although Curcic no longer smiled like a circus ringmaster, his expression wasn't as sombre as that of his disciples. 'This is a glad day!' he boomed, arms spread wide as he turned away from the crucifixes and addressed his people. 'I was once a sinner, as you all know. Then I was found, like a little lost lamb. Baptised in blood, not water, for we are the chosen few. Our Lord has forsaken the rest, because they were unrepentant. Today, we welcome more penitents. And they welcome His holy absolution.' He cocked his head to one side. 'Bring forth the blood of Our Lord.'

A strapping man heaved a wooden barrel across the grass, placed it close to the penitent and prised free the lid.

A tall woman fetched a ladle and presented it to Curcic.

John's healing arm was burning; he was desperate to relax his posture. His nose wrinkled as Curcic plunged a ladle into the red liquid. Even from five metres away, the iron scent was strong. It was just a bit of blood, though. They would play along, pretend to become devout followers, then steal away in the dead of night. Hopefully, their motorcycles remained undamaged. With a little finesse, they could convince Curcic of their gratitude for showing them the light. For protecting them from zombs, bikers and Comanches.

Each baptism – a spoonful of blood splashed over the head – was accompanied by the following sentence: 'O Lord, in your infinite wisdom, cleanse these souls with the blood of your son, that they may be absolved of sin and be permitted to spread your word.'

Every time it was uttered, the congregation said, 'Amen' in reply.

Curcic's mirth had been replaced by a solemn fervour. John wondered whether or not the man truly believed. Was he like Silas, exploiting and lying to further his own interests? Perhaps he was simply insane.

'Thus concludes part one of the ceremony,' Curcic said after splashing Cyril with blood.

John relaxed his arms a touch.

'And now, the second and final stage of acceptance.'

Sniffing the air, John scented a familiar smell. For a moment he looked for Frank, but the bot was locked in one of the town Sheriff Department's cells.

Curcic continued, 'Our Saviour, Jesus Christ, shed blood for our sins. He sacrificed his own life to save many. Followers of Christ must do the same.' He turned away from his flock and addressed his new recruits. 'Which of you will follow His example?'

John gulped; his stomach sank.

The Aug-Frees glanced at one another with wide eyes.

'One of you must die today. But fear not, for your humility will be rewarded. You will be immediately accepted into God's Kingdom. Heaven awaits. One of you must stand, now, and accept God's judgment.'

None of the Aug-Frees moved.

'Blood must be shed. Make your choice now, or I will choose one of you at random.'

The man was a psychopath. Staring at him and beseeching him for mercy was sure to be fruitless, but the kneeling nine tried anyway.

Their pleas were ignored. 'Very well.' Curcic's bejewelled teeth glinted in the sunlight. 'I will choose.' He studied the AFs. The wind ruffled his coiffured hair.

And there it was again. The indescribable miasma raised the hackles on John's neck. Now it was accompanied by a low rumble, a continuous earthquake which came closer with every heartbeat.

'You.' Curcic pointed at Curls. 'You are young, pure. Or,' he paused, the twinkle in his eyes matching that of his grin, 'at least, you *look* pure.' He raised a hand.

A group of men, about forty-strong, stepped forwards from the front rank of Pro-Churchers. Their faces were blank, their fists clenched. Most of them restrained the eight Aug-Frees who hadn't been marked for death.

As John was wrestled to the ground, he yelled. Not in protest at his own fate, however – it was the panic in Curls's eyes as she was gagged and dragged away from her friends that stirred him. 'Let her go!' he demanded again, receiving a kick to the ribs for his trouble. He just about saw Vincente being manhandled to the ground. A maniacal woman, a knife in her hand, slit the Puerto Rican's throat. Arterial spray soaked the grass.

Fear overcame revulsion and sharpened John's senses. An inferno of pain in his injured arm. Thuds, curses, grunts and, in the background, cries of encouragement from Curcic's minions. The dampness of soil on John's cheek. A weighty boot at the base of his skull, pinning him like a skewered pig. Warm blood in his mouth, sweet but sour. And that creeping stench of decay, growing stronger by the minute.

Suddenly there were screams. Female at first, but soon, deeper voices were calling in panic.

'Fall back to the Church!' Curcic roared.

The pressure on John's neck disappeared. Coughing, he scrambled to his feet and watched the fanatics flee, while his comrades rose to their feet. They gaped. He turned, and he saw. 'Run!' he shouted. His first few steps were in reverse, tentative ones as he blinked in shock. There was a T-junction fifty metres to the east of the square. From the right-hand arm of the T, a host of zomb-augs approached. Thousands of the things, as if a sports arena full of them had been emptied into the town. As one they lurched towards the humans who were yet to run. With grey-tinted flesh, grasping hands and slack mouths they came, jostling for position.

The hunt had begun.

Chapter 25

John's legs pounded; his arms pumped. The pain in his bicep was forgotten.

His friends sprinted, following Amber. Unlike Curcic's crew, they weren't headed for the church. Their Harleys were, hopefully, still intact at the vehicle charging station half a kilometre from the town hall.

'Wait!' John shouted when they'd travelled about 300m. He stopped and leaned on his knees, blowing hard.

The others slowed to a jog. 'What?' said Amber, watching their rear. They'd turned a couple of corners; the zombs were no longer in sight.

'I need to get Frank.'

'Fuck that!' Cyril and Gideon said in unison. They broke into a run once more.

John spat. 'I'll go on my own, then.' He looked around. Hoping for a sign to the Sheriff's Department, he was disappointed. But they'd explored the town centre's environs the previous evening and had passed the building in question. He just needed a minute to get his bearings.

'No,' said Amber, 'you won't. We're coming with.'

Juarez had followed the two brothers. Curls hesitated, her eyes wide, before sprinting to catch up with Juarez. Amber, Cait and T were with John.

'It's down there,' Cait said.

'You sure?' John pointed to the south. 'I thought it was the other way.'

Cait was already jogging northwards.

'Trust her,' said T. 'She's good at this shit.'

A gunshot sounded, and then another, from the north. Then a ragged burst of automatic fire and the distant sound of screams. Smoke was drifting across the sky to the south.

Just then, the fastest zombies came into view. Those at the front began to lurch and vocalise, their arms already outstretched despite being thirty metres from their prey. They filled the avenue, like a sick parade with no spectators.

With Cait leading the way, the AFs covered a couple of blocks. At one point, their intended route was foiled by another mass of zombs. Eventually, however, they reached the Department, on Wilson Street. The tree-lined boulevard was deserted. T gave the old door a couple of kicks. Glass smashed and wood splintered. Entry was made. As an afterthought, Cait shut the door behind them and pushed a desk up against it.

It was a small station; it didn't take long to locate the jail. Frank was already halfway free. The steel bars were creaking in his hands as he struggled to prise them apart. On a desk against one wall was a set of keys. After a couple of minutes and a lot of fiddling, they selected the correct key. Frank was released.

'Right,' said Amber. 'Time to go.'

A quick glance through the front window confirmed their fears: a significant number of zomb-augs were outside. The four humans and the cyborg dropped to a squat.

'The back?' T hissed. 'I don't think they know we're here.'

The others nodded.

Through the Department they went. They moved in a half-crouch, lest they be spotted through the window. The rear door, which was criss-crossed with thick wooden slats to keep out intruders, was in a room adjacent to the jail. A couple of hammers and a half-empty box of nails were on the ground. As they attacked the beams reinforcing the door, they heard another crash from the front of the building. Suddenly, the groans and footfalls of the undead were louder.

'They're in,' John whispered, prying another nail free from the timber whilst wiping sweat from his brow.

T wielded the other hammer.

Amber, Frank and Cait were helping to loosen the nails by pulling on the planks.

One beam remained when the first zomb appeared through the door. It'd once been a short, balding man. Now it was a grey-skinned, shaky-legged, blood-splattered horror. Jaw flexing, fingers twitching, head lolling. Upon seeing the would-be escapees, its amble became a strut.

Frank grabbed a fallen two-by-four and stepped forwards.

From a metre away the monster dived at its adversary.

But the android was too quick. His sidestep left the zomb clutching at nothing. The downwards chop of his weapon crushed skull like ripe fruit.

Meanwhile, Cait rushed to close the internal door. An arm slipped through, however. Although Cait and then Amber heaved until veins were visible in their foreheads, they couldn't dislodge the scrawny appendage. More hands slithered through the crack. The crack became 15cm; 15cm became 30cm. John lent his weight. Even so, new arms, and even legs, appeared, as if a giant squid were forcing entry.

'Got it!' T's voice was followed by a clunk of wood hitting floor and a delicious breeze.

'Go!' Frank had a plank in each hand. 'I'll delay them in here for a moment while you get a head start. I'll catch you up.'

T, Cait and Amber fled. John paused for a moment, a protest on his lips. He left in pursuit of his friends, glancing over his shoulder to see the unblocked internal door burst open. Out in the alleyway, he heard multiple consecutive thuds from inside the building.

'Run!' Frank called, his tone surreally placid.

John broke into a jog. His arm had begun to protest. The others were twenty metres away, about to turn left at the end of the alley. A dozen zombs approached from the opposite direction.

'Come on, John!' Amber yelled, risking a fleeting look his way. She and Cait both carried two-by-fours, and they were bracing themselves to strike. T was ready with his hammer. As John closed the distance, zomb-augs appeared. The women swung; T hacked; the freaks fell. John sprinted, arriving just in time to help repel more zombs. He copied T, aiming for the eyes and using lots of quick shots instead of big swings. Whacking the creatures was both satisfying and disturbing, and it took more strength than he remembered.

They could either turn left or right. To the left, fifteen metres away, the main body of zombies passed on Wilson Street, most of them unaware of the humans nearby. A tantalisingly empty street was to the right.

'What about Frank?' John asked, hesitating.

'He can look after himself.' Amber ran right.

As did the others.

John waited a few more seconds, until a handful of zombs on Wilson Street espied him and lurched his way. Cursing, he darted in pursuit of his friends.

The rest of the way was danger-free. Presumably, the bulk of the invading force was occupied by the Pro-Church army. Frequent gunshots suggested the latter was resisting. When Amber's detachment arrived at the charge station, they were surprised by Cyril, Gideon and Curls, who'd been hiding in the kiosk. From somewhere the two brothers had each acquired a gun. Greetings were not exchanged.

'Where's Juarez?' Amber asked.

'The guys who had these guns shot him,' Gideon said. 'Don't worry, they got what was coming to them.'

T and Cait swore. Amber blew a long breath.

'Bikes ain't here,' the eldest brother stated.

'Shit,' said Amber.

'But we found a big old RV out back,' Cyril enthused. 'Fully charged, ready to dust.'

'Excellent,' said Cait in a detached manner.

A lengthy barrage of gunfire sounded from the town centre. Abruptly, Gideon and Cyril turned and stalked away, heading for the rear of the station shop.

'Wait a minute.' John's feet were planted. 'We need to wait for Frank.'

'Bullshit.' Gideon didn't stop walking. 'Fuck him, the freaks will be here in no time.'

'Yeah.' Cyril expectorated. 'We're going now. You wanna stay here, that's your business.'

John felt Amber's, T's and Cait's eyes on him, but he continued to stare at the siblings' backs. 'Stop!' he exclaimed, his temper lost.

Gideon continued, his only response a rude gesture.

Cyril spun on his heel. 'Or what?' Although he wasn't pointing his rifle at John, he wasn't pointing it away from him, either. 'What you gonna do, robot-lover?'

'Just… give him five minutes, please.'

Cyril raised his gun.

'Woah, woah,' Amber said. 'Relax, Cyril, lower the gun.'

Gideon stopped and, mouth agape, faced his brother.

At first John felt terror. Then he realised that the weapon's barrel was not aimed at him. Something else was in the crosshairs.

'Look!' T waved with both arms.

John twisted.

It was Frank, a hundred metres away. Hurrying towards the group, he still carried two wooden planks; both were cracked and bloodied.

'It's a zomb!' Gideon drew his pistol.

Cyril fired.

John exclaimed.

Frank ducked. The first bullet missed its mark. The cyborg began to sprint, but he was limping. Shot number two hit an upside down car.

'What the fuck?' John inched towards the pair. 'That's Frank!'

Grinning, Gideon fired two rounds of his own. 'Looks like a freak to me.'

Another successful dodge. Frank was within 50m.

Cyril dropped to one knee and squinted.

Part of John was inclined to rush the bastard and seize his weapon, but he feared taking the shot meant for Frank. And this one flew true. John gasped as his bot went down.

Enraged, he launched himself at Cyril, grabbing the rifle with both hands.

Chapter 26

'Hey!' Gideon had his pistol pointed at John. 'Back up, now, or I shoot you in the face.'

John seethed. He loosened his hold on Cyril's gun but didn't move.

'Stand down, Gideon!' Amber ordered.

'When he backs up I will.'

Though tempted to headbutt Cyril, John swallowed and turned away.

T and Cait stared at the brothers with hard eyes.

'Let's all be cool,' Amber said. 'Be cool.' She waited a moment.

John's shoulders slumped; his head bowed.

The siblings watched him, their expressions inscrutable.

Suddenly cold, John walked over to Frank. He knelt next to his companion. The hole in his leg shouldn't have been enough to kill him, but he was completely still. In his peripheral vision, John saw movement. Zomb-augs were headed their way. 'Come on, Frank. I built you tougher than this.'

'I know you did,' Frank whispered.

John started.

'I'm playing dead, so they don't shoot me again. Don't let them see you reply.'

His lips barely moving, John said, 'There are zombs headed our way.'

'I know. Judging by the vibrations in the ground, they'll be upon us within the next couple of minutes. So pretend I'm dead and go. I'll catch you up.'

'John?' Cait called. 'We got company. Need to leave.'

'Okay.' John stood. He winked at Frank, who returned the gesture.

Rain began to fall. At least a hundred zomb-augs had emerged from the road leading to the town centre. Even from fifty metres, the fresh blood of Curcic's people was visible on their clothes. It was time to leave.

***

Packed into the recreational vehicle – from which all furnishings had been removed, leaving an empty shell – the AF's were quiet. T was driving. Curls appeared bashful. Amber and Cait were furious, especially the latter, who'd had her arms tied behind her back because of her "attitude." Gideon and Cyril were nonchalant.

After ten minutes of silence, Amber spoke: 'So what exactly happened to Juarez?'

Curls turned away, her face pale.

'Told you.' Cyril clucked his tongue. 'He got shot.'

'Do you not know what "exactly" means?' Cait asked.

'Listen.' Gideon tapped his knee with his pistol. 'About time you showed some respect. We got new rules. New management.'

'What the fuck you talking about?' Amber leaned forwards.

'Us.' Cyril patted his rifle butt. '*We're* in charge now. We got the guns, we run the show.' He smirked, then glanced towards the front of the van. 'Yo, T, think we can speed it up a bit? We're crawling, here.'

'Negative,' T replied. 'Got some kinda power-restrictor fitted.'

'Fucksake,' Gideon said.

'You in a rush, *boss*?' Cait said with disdain.

'You betcha. See, Silas told the big chiefs all about me and my bro. Said we'd be "valuable assets" to them, you know?'

'Damn right,' chimed Cyril. 'Silas planned to meet the bikers, but he left things open with the people in Charleston. So that's where we're going.'

'You think they'll be down with this?' Cait asked.

'Sure.' Gideon gave a gap-toothed grin. 'They'll see we got a few unruly comrades under control. We'll tell them we got rid of the android. All goes in our favour, don't it?'

'Bullshit,' Amber spat. 'They'll see you for what you are, couple of redneck morons with delusions of grandeur.'

'Watch yourself, little lady.' Gideon rapped his leg with the gun again. 'Like I said, bit of respect. Start to show it, or there'll be trouble.'

John bristled; Cait strained against her bonds.

Amber just rolled her eyes.

'Why are we stopping?' Curls said.

T had parked next to a burnt-out dumper truck.

'Some kinda battery problem,' T called. 'Maybe it ain't a power-restrictive. Gonna get out and take a look. John, you're handy with tools, wanna help?' Without waiting for a response, he climbed out of the RV.

Shrugging, John pulled the sliding door open.

'Woah!' Gideon said. 'Cyril's going too, case you get any funny ideas.'

Led by the younger brother, John decamped. His feet squelched in thick mud. The pair met T, who'd already raised the van's hood.

Cyril kept a few metres distance between himself and his subordinates, and he held his rifle across his chest. He leaned his back against the truck's blackened cab. 'No fucking about, you hear?'

Gideon said something similar to those still in the camper.

T was focussed on the exposed engine.

John gave Cyril a withering look and joined his friend. 'Looks okay to me.'

'You sure?' T said loudly. Then, in a whisper, 'Whisper back to me.'

'Whisper what?' John murmured.

'Anything. Just say it quietly.'

'Okay. Like this?'

'Yeah, like that.'

'Right. Why, what are we doing? What —'

'Hey!' Cyril warned. 'What you two whispering about?'

John and T turned to protest their innocence.

Eyes narrowed, Cyril took two steps in their direction. 'Quit fooling around and get it fixed. Quick, now, because —'

A flurry of movement. From behind the eighteen-wheeler came a bipedal figure. Although Cyril swivelled, he was too slow. The humanoid knocked him off his feet.

It was Frank.

The boss easily wrested the rifle from Cyril's hands and used its stock to stun his foe. Then he pointed the longarm at the RV.

'Fuck's going on?' Gideon said from inside the van. His face bobbed into view. When he saw the gun aimed at his head, he blanched.

'Toss your weapon to the floor and come out with your hands up.' Frank spoke as if they were words he frequently uttered.

Gideon complied with the second order. But not the first. Without the use of his hands, he awkwardly stepped out of the vehicle. The pistol was pointing skywards.

'He said, "toss your weapon,"' John reminded.

Gideon ignored him. 'Where the fuck did he come from?'

Amber and Curls were now watching events.

'He's been clinging to the top of the vehicle.' T grinned. 'That's why I was driving slow.'

'Drop the gun, Gideon,' Frank repeated. 'Or I'll blow your hand off. No sudden movements.'

Gideon nodded. He began to gradually lower his hands.

Suddenly, Frank tripped – Cyril had regained consciousness and grabbed him by the ankle. As the cyborg fell, he fired. Gideon's head jerked backwards. There was a sharp crack as the slug struck the underside of the RV's roof.

Amber and Curls were sprayed with fragments of skull, flesh and brain. The former clutched her eyes and cursed in agony.

Crimson poured from a hole in Gideon's forehead. His eyes frozen open, he fell to his knees. With a roar of anguish, Cyril scrabbled across the ground, reaching for the sidearm his brother had dropped. T moved to intercept, but he slipped on the sodden soil and landed heavily.

'No!' John cried as he dived. He landed on Cyril, winding himself. Somehow, he found the strength to wrap an arm around the bereft sibling's throat. His grip slackened when one of Cyril's elbows hit his nose. Eyes watering, John tasted blood.

'Freeze, you murdering bastard,' Curls said. The click of a pistol's safety switch was audible.

Cyril's struggles stopped. He began to shake and sob.

T stood up gingerly. He was nursing his left wrist.

Amber, covering one of her eyes, and holding the length of dirty rope used on Cait, climbed out of the van. She tied Cyril's hands behind his back and sighed.

John released Cyril and allowed Amber to pull him upright. He wiped blood from his nostrils, lips and chin before helping Frank to stand.

The bot was covered in dirt.

Cait, newly-freed, put her arm around Curls's shoulders.

Apart from Cyril, who was weeping and muttering, everyone was silent. No one looked at Gideon's corpse or the pool of blood in which he lay. Or his stricken brother in the mud.

John caught Curls's eye – she'd finally lowered Gideon's pistol – and gave her a nod of thanks. Then, mouth agape, he pointed at her.

She frowned. Of course, she couldn't see the laser dot dancing on her sternum.

T, Amber and Cait were laser-targeted, too. All three were unaware of their predicament until they looked at each other and saw the little red lights.

John and Frank spun on their heels. Three snipers were atop the crashed truck. Two were in the cabin. One lay under the lorry. They wore military fatigues, had paint on their faces; they carried big, modern guns. Unblinking, the soldiers stared at the Aug-Frees like cats at fledgling sparrows.

There was a thud and a squelch from the tail end of the vehicle-cum-fort. And footsteps. A squat, square-faced man appeared. He held a pistol, but he approached, smiling, as if walking in the park. 'Are we interrupting something?' he asked in an educated voice.

Chapter 27

So, they were prisoners.

Amber said not. In her mind, the Aug-Frees should wait to be presented to President Blanchflower before they formulated an opinion. Perhaps all outsiders were treated this way, she suggested. Blindfolded and manacled, bundled into a personnel carrier and driven to an unknown location by muscular, black-clad paramilitaries. What was worrying about that?

At least they were safe, said Curls. These men and women appeared more than capable of protecting them from zombies, bikers, Pro-Churchers, Comanches and anyone else. The initial standoff aside, they'd shown no aggression towards the NYC AFs thus far. Wasn't that reassuring?

And they were AugFrees, just like their newest guests. Cait wasn't given to unwarranted optimism, but Blanchflower was a president, which implied democracy. Said president's people seemed committed to her cause without being crazed zealots. Their cautious practices meant they were thorough, not threatening. Didn't they?

Cyril was being treated for shock. Judging by his snores, he'd been sedated.

Frank was quiet.

The journey was short, so neither T nor John had time to express their opinions. The former's body language was obscured by the hood on John's head. But his silence, save for the occasional sigh or tut, spoke volumes: like John, he was anxious.

They'd travelled for no more than ten kilometres when the vehicle halted. There was a faint sound of hydraulics. The clanking of steel. Then the bus began to move once more. Except that this time, it was travelling on a steep, downwards gradient, and the temperature was rising. When the personnel carrier ceased again, there was a louder, closer metallic noise; the hatch at the rear had been opened.

'Right,' a cheery voice announced. 'The end of the line.'

Somebody walked down the centre aisle of the passenger section, bumping John's knees. 'Up, up!' His voice was Hispanic. 'You, wake up. Come on, the President's waiting.'

John stood. He shuffled in the direction of the bus's back entrance.

'Watch the drop,' the Latino man said.

Too late for John, who stumbled as he stepped onto a ramp. Murmuring an expletive, he continued to tread carefully until he reached solid ground.

'Okay,' cheerful man said. 'Hoods off.'

'Jesus!' T exclaimed. 'Too bright!'

John's mask was removed. He'd closed his eyes in preparation. He opened them by degrees to allow his pupils to adjust. Amber was stood to his left, shielding her face; there was no one to his right. They stood in a line, in the centre of a hangar the size of a football field. Happy man was grey-headed, tall and paced the floor with his arms behind his back. Hispanic man was younger, shorter, stockier. He was standing to attention, his pock-marked face weary. Both wore the same uniforms as the ambushers who'd captured the AFs. Each had a rifle strapped to his back.

At one end of the chamber was a large shuttered exit, possibly used for vehicular access. Nearby was a standard-sized door. It opened, and through it sauntered a business-suited woman of average height and athletic build.

Everyone apart from the servicemen watched the brunette as she approached. Her heels, surreally loud, made the only noise in the hangar.

When she reached the newcomers, she stopped and looked at each person in turn. Her face was ageless, her expression inscrutable. 'Greetings. Thank you for coming.' Her accent was neutral, as was her tone. 'I am Blanchflower of the AugFrees. You are not prisoners, you are guests. Valued guests, whose stay is, for now, mandatory. You will be treated well. You will be fed. Your injuries will be treated. In return for our hospitality, you will respect our laws and customs.' She smiled thinly. 'Are there any questions?'

Nobody answered.

'Excellent. We will get to know each other better, soon. Until then, I bid you good day.'

So, they *were* prisoners.